D1614764

EMERGING
BUTTERFLY

EMERGING
BUTTERFLY

A MEMOIR

CONSTANCE G. JONES

This memoir is a work of creative nonfiction. Many names and identifying details have been changed to maintain anonymity and protect the privacy of the people involved. I have done my best to recreate events, locales, and conversations from my memories of them; they are real to the extent of my knowledge and to the point that they can accurately convey their essence.

Edited By Angela Panayotopulos
thewritequality.worpress.com

Cover & Book Design: mycustombookcover.com

ISBN: 978-1-7338439-0-4 (Hardcover)

ISBN: 978-1-7338439-1-1 (Paperback)

ISBN: 978-1-7338439-2-8 (eBook)

Library of Congress Control Number: 2019903549

First Printed in United States 2019

Beautiful Sky Publishing
P.O. Box 235840
Encinitas, CA 92023

DEDICATION

I dedicate this book to my readers…you may face many struggles in your life as did I, and feel at times that you can't go on, but you can and you will because you are never alone. Never be afraid to ask for help because there are people in this world who care about you. I hope that my story inspires you to continue moving forward toward the life that you imagine for yourself. You and only you can make it happen.

Thanks be to God for protecting, loving, and guiding my footsteps along the way.

ACKNOWLEDGMENTS

It takes a village to write a book, and with the size of my tribe, I had a tremendous amount of support.

First I'd like to thank my husband and best friend, Claude. Since the day we met seven years ago, my heart's been yours. You are my biggest supporter and fan. I love you for always being there for me. You inspire me to be better each day. Your encouragement during some of the most difficult times helped me keep moving forward towards my dream of sharing my story with the world. I am eternally grateful and feel so blessed to have you in my life. Thank you for all you do. I am forever "In It to Win It" with you.

To my editor, Angela Panayotopulos—A huge thanks to you for your hard work, guidance, and support. Your collaboration and partnership was amazing. You taught me that even the smallest of details make such a difference in a book. You and I spent quite a bit of time together and I want to let you know that I now consider you not just an editor, but a friend—and I look forward to working with you again on my next book! I know this is just the beginning for us.

Mom—Thank you for sticking it out with us kids. It wasn't easy for me growing up in our family, but I know you did your best to provide for us. We never went hungry, always had a roof over our heads, and there was love. Your heart is enormous—and I know it had to be to love nine children while raising them alone. I was not always the most tactful child and I had a strong mind and will; I still do. Yes, *stubborn* is the word that comes to mind. You loved me anyway. I know our relationship has faced its challenges in the past, but we have come so far and I am thankful that we are closer now. I know I can call on you for love, support, and guidance. Thanks for answering all my questions during the writing process. Thank you for loving me and making an effort to be in my life.

Grandma—You embodied strength. You didn't take shit from anybody and I loved that about you most. You made sure I always had a birthday cake and dress when I was a little girl, and you would take me away for the weekend so I could spend time with you and Jim. Those weekends gave me much-needed breathing space away from the craziness of home.

To my sisters—All three of you are so special to me. Through the writing of this book and our many conversations, I was able to see your takes on growing up in the Grays household and how my life impacted yours. Thank you for allowing my life to be an example of what you can achieve when you align your mind and actions. I am proud of you, and forever grateful for your unconditional love and the unbreakable bond we share.

To my brothers—I was the only girl smashed between four of you for quite some time, and that's a lot of testosterone to deal with… but I wouldn't have it any other way. I had to be strong to keep up with you boys, which probably explains my love of Wonder Woman as a child. Knowing I had brothers I could count on to keep me safe in scary times made all the difference. I am here today because you were strong for me when I needed it most. I love you all.

To the rest of my tribe—There are too many of you to count, but you all made room for me in your lives. To my aunts and uncles who made sure I had new clothes to wear on my first day of school and who took me to places I would otherwise be unable to go: thank you. I am forever grateful to my cousins, who included me in their lives and their adventures. You all did what you could to make me feel special and loved. I appreciate you; I truly hope this book is testament to that.

To all of my friends, near and far, I want you to know that you have all touched my life at different stages and I am so grateful. You know who you are and I hope, as you're reading this book, you will understand how much your lives impacted mine for the better. A special thanks to my dear friends who took time to read my book during the writing process and gave me invaluable feedback to enrich it further. I appreciate you all.

I can't forget Mr. D., Chris Daniels, and all the teachers and mentors who guided me and provided rays of hope and love throughout my journey. By watching you, I caught a glimpse of what life was like outside of my chaotic setting—and what life *could be*. Perhaps you'll never know how powerfully that helped shape my view of the world and my perception of myself. You saw potential in me and you went out of your way to let me know I was special. A part of the reason I am where I am in life today is because of you.

Thank you.

CONTENTS

PART I
1980–1987

"For in every adult there dwells the child that was, and in
every child there lies the adult that will be."

—John Connolly, *The Book of Lost Things*

FATHER WOLF

A child should never have to choose between opening the door for her father and having her heart broken.

I should know. I had to.

My mother ran out to the store one Saturday evening back in the spring of 1986, leaving me and two of my younger brothers behind in the little two-bedroom apartment we called home. Her qualms were lessened by the fact that her sister lived down the stairs in the same apartment complex, which meant that us kids had someone to turn to in case of an emergency.

Before my mother left, she gave me specific instructions.

She crouched down and faced me, grabbing my shoulders to ensure that I was paying attention. "There are some things going on between your daddy and me," she said. "You saw what happened the other day. I don't think it's safe for him to come into the house." Her eyes shone bright in her freckled face. Her untamable hair, naturally red and curly, frizzed around her head like a frazzled halo. "If he comes by, no matter what he says, do not open the door. I don't want him here, do you understand? I don't want anything to happen to you. I don't want him to take you kids from me."

My heart pounded at the thought of such a confrontation. I nodded.

"Constance, do you promise? Say it."

"I promise," I whispered.

Mommy caressed my cheek before she stood up and grabbed her purse. Her eyes met mine once more before she left. "No matter what he says," she repeated, "don't let him in."

Later in life, I would come across a fairy tale of seven little goats that are left alone at home after their mother leaves to go scavenge for food to bring back. Before the mother goat leaves, she warns her kids to keep the door locked and to be very careful, since there are rumors of a wolf prowling around the area. The wolf indeed comes house-calling once Mother Goat leaves. The little goats refuse to open the door to him, recognizing that he is not their mother. The wolf retreats, disguises himself by whitening his paws with flour and masking his rough voice, and returns to the house; this time, he tricks the little goats into thinking that he is their mother. When the goats open the door, he eats them. In most versions of this fairy tale, the mother goat hunts down the wolf and cuts open his belly while he sleeps, rescuing her kids and filling the wolf's belly with seven rocks before he awakens.

It only took fifteen minutes for Daddy to show up.

The image of my father's face in the tiny rectangular window that flanked one side of our home's front door haunts me to this day. I remember how his eyes attempted to meet mine, red-rimmed with alcohol and shadowed by his demons. He braced himself against the door with one hand, the beer in his system tricking him into believing that the world was spinning faster than he was.

"Connie!" he exclaimed when he saw me. "My Connie-coo…how are you doing?" A big grin split his face, a sight that both warmed my heart and gutted my stomach. It was like a surreal nightmare, the sort where you meet someone you love and realize that their teeth have been replaced by daggers when they smile back at you in greeting. "I haven't seen you in a while…let Daddy inside."

I shook my head. I don't know if I could smell the rancid scent of stale beer on his breath, but I sure as hell would have been able to imagine it. It had become as familiar a scent as his aftershave.

My father was a tall man—a head taller than my mother, though he seemed to tower even higher in my six-year-old eyes. He could carry himself with poise; when he wore his suit and his sobriety, he was nothing short of distinguished. His brown eyes could be as warm and mellow as sun-kissed honey. He could speak with an undeniable charisma that earned him job positions (though he was always quickly fired) and that would eventually help him gain a following as a pastor. Until I was six years old, I was convinced that my father could move mountains.

His posture was not poised that evening. His voice was not charismatic. But he was Daddy, and pieces of my heart began to crumble with every stubborn shake of my head.

"Wha's wrong?" He slurred his words as if someone had implanted a voice-changing device into his throat that warped his speech. "Come on, let me in. I jus' wanna talk. Let me in so I can see you and give you a hug. I missed you, baby."

A part of me really wanted to. My daddy was no wolf. I wanted to open the door and let him sweep me into his arms and give me a kiss and tell me that everything was okay, that I didn't have to be strong and lonely and mature all the time. I wanted him to hang around and apologize to Mommy and tuck me into bed at night after reading to me from one of my favorite Dr. Seuss books. But a bigger part of me knew that he wouldn't. A bigger part of me was terrified that Mommy was right. If I opened the door, maybe my father would kidnap us. Maybe he would hurt Mommy. Maybe he *was* the wolf.

My little brothers, playing in the bedroom and out of sight, remained oblivious to the situation. I could hear the clacking of the building blocks as they toppled and the boys' laughter as they grabbed their toy cars and made *zoom zoom* noises while pushing the rubber wheels against the carpet. I had to be the strong one. I had to keep the door shut.

"I can't," I said.

"Why not? Why can't you let me in the house?"

"Mommy said you can't come in."

"Oh, it's okay, Connie-coo…your mommy didn't really mean that." His bleary eyes begged me. Their darkness frightened me. "It's okay."

Except it wasn't okay, and I knew it. Emotions whirled inside me like a tornado, my love for my father fueling my hatred and grudge against him that he'd put me in this position, that he couldn't be the daddy I wanted and needed. My heartbeat quickened, fluttering like a butterfly wing. Separated from him by a glass pane and a locked wooden door, I began to weep.

When my father noticed the silent tears streaming down my face, he changed his tune.

"Oh, honey…okay, okay, I see that I'm upsetting you." His face softened as he gazed at me. "It's okay," he repeated. "It's okay, baby…I'm gonna go now. Jus' tell your mom that I came by…"

It's okay…it's okay… His words lingered with me as I watched him stumble away from the door, down the steps and out of sight through the veil of my tears. *It's okay…*

My mother arrived home later that evening to find me shaking like a leaf. When I told her what had happened, she apologized and hugged me as the reality of the situation kicked in and noisy sobs racked my body. "It's okay," she murmured, attempting to soothe me, trying to make us both believe the lie. "It's okay…"

It wasn't okay. It wasn't the first time my father had shown up drunk. It wasn't the first time he'd left us for days on end after having a horrific fight with my mother, his eyes narrowed to slits or dangerously rimmed red. Though he never hit us kids, I'd witnessed him abusing my mom multiple times, and her bruises and black eyes wouldn't let me overlook the facts. I'd seen the police cars and uniformed men who knocked on our door from time to time and took him away for domestic abuse.

Yet this was the same man who read me stories, shooed away the monsters beneath my bed, and filled my days with hugs and laughter. He was the one who called me his "little princess," who always wanted me to play outside in pants and long-sleeved shirts so I wouldn't scrape or scar my skin as I rode my bike or chased butterflies. This was the man who transported me with his gentle recitations of *Oh! The Places You'll Go!* He was the one whom I sang and danced for; my mother would later tell me that I had developed my own special ritual that I shared only with Daddy: a five-minute-long getting-ready-for-sleep dance, where I'd dance in place and chortle an unintelligible song in happy baby-talk before being tucked into bed.

My mind couldn't rationalize that my father could be all of those people. How could someone be both Father Goat and Father Wolf? How could that possibly be okay?

Throughout my childhood, I would make notes in my diary regarding the truths that I uncovered, jotting them down like commandments. *You can't trust men. Do not have kids if you cannot afford them. Never let a man beat you. Don't force your kids to act as parents. Make sure you make enough money. Prioritize dignity and decency.* I would come to realize that what a person *can* do and what he or she actually *does* might be as dissimilar as night and day.

And no, that's not okay.

BUTTERFLY GIRL

If there's one thing I've learned in my thirty-nine years of life thus far, it's this: you can take the stones that life flings at you and you can do whatever you want with them. You can allow them to knock you down and bury you beneath the rubble, or you can put them together and build yourself a beautiful castle. You can't choose where or when you're born or what you're born into. That's not something you control. That is your gift or your curse, and can haunt you to your dying day like an evil godmother's spell. But, like any such spell, it can also be broken.

You can break it.

You can thwart it.

You can do something about it.

You always have a choice in *that*.

The question is: what do you choose to do?

If you, my friend, decided to pay us a visit—an African-American family surviving in the heart and heat of San Diego in the early 1980s—I'm curious what you would make of us. You would knock on the flimsy blue door of our second-floor apartment and would be welcomed into a cramped set of rooms with threadbare brown carpets and sun-bleached curtains. You would be seated on the second-hand velvet sofa and offered a cold glass of grape Kool-Aid—in a plastic glass, of course; I think my siblings had broken all the glass ones we ever had by the time I was born.

Do you enjoy fairy tales? You would have found a modern-day Rapunzel in the form of my mother, a woman with long, lush red hair who was trapped in a tower of terror for most of her life. In our version of the story, my mother—Evonne Grays—was one of seven children, a magic number in most fairy tales. Her parents relished the company of alcohol; their choice of poison consumed and possessed them, fueling domestic fights and abuse. After my grandmother finally packed herself and her seven kids up and fled from Detroit to San Diego, my fourteen-year-old mother was insecure and reckless. She had trouble adjusting to a new life in California. Her unique beauty—finely chiseled features, naturally auburn hair, a sweet face with freckles and dimples—made her vulnerable. Two husbands and nine children later, she would partially break free of the mental prison-tower of her fears, but how do you say goodbye to your demons when they've become closer than your shadow?

You probably wouldn't get a chance to meet my father, because I'm almost positive that he wouldn't be home when you came visiting. Sylvester Grays was also one of seven children, born of a mother who committed suicide before his seventh birthday and a father who once beat him so mercilessly that he was found in a pool of blood and taken to a hospital. A rough childhood of foster care, drug-dealing, and gang involvement resulted in my father's lifelong love affair with the bottle. If alcohol could talk, I know what whispered promises it would have made him: *I'm your one true friend. I'll never leave you. I'll always be here for you. I'll be your most faithful companion till the day you die.*

But, my friend, you would have met us, the children—the number of children you'd meet depending on what year you'd visit. My eldest siblings, unpredictable Mia (a schizophrenic since early adolescence) and unsmiling Andre (emerging as a bully due to the battlefield of his childhood), were from my mother's first marriage, a violent backstory that was imprinted on their characters. When my mother married my father, they had Derrick, a cheerful boy who would grow into a solemn man; throughout early childhood, he turned out to be my strongest ally and closest friend. Two years later, they had me. Two years later, they had my pensive brother Michael. And the two-year pattern persisted: fiery Jeremiah, then hustling Xavier, then darling Alyssa, and finally—only one year later—baby Laila.

Seven children together; nine in total.

I suppose you could say that my siblings and I had a fairytale element of our own in our daily struggle to survive, subconsciously seeking any type of magic that would enable us to cultivate a beanstalk or summon a magic carpet. I have never planted a beanstalk, never ridden a magic carpet, and my real-life godmother (who was neither magical nor fashion-forward as those in fairy tales, but who loved me nonetheless) disappeared after leaving my uncle when I was about five years old. It took a few decades, but I came to realize that magic carpets and beanstalks—had they even shown up at my door—wouldn't be able to change my life unless I accepted them as a manifestation of transformations.

And transformations are an inside job.

The Beginning

I was born a queen.

Okay, not exactly. But I imagine my father would have liked the idea, given the name that he chose for me. So let's backtrack to the beginning. Well, *my* beginning anyway.

Soon before I was born, my parents separated for the fifth time; my father had snuck out of the house to go drink, and my mother confronted him one night upon his return. Their shouting frightened my older siblings and a couple of my cousins who were sleeping over. My mother gave her usual ultimatum, packed her bags, and called her sister—my Aunt Ledesi—to come take her and the kids away. My dad passed out on the bed. The next day, he called up a friend, who took him to the airport, where he fled to LA, lurking there for the next few months. He arrived back in San Diego for the occasion of my birth, a week before I appeared.

When I came into the world, my family was already a sizeable tribe of people, though some relatives lived further away than others. There was my mother's sister Ledesi, a clipped-voiced teacher and a voice of reason, who lived alone with her kids (Sanaa and Nala) in the same apartment complex as us. There was my mother's brother Kahari, the professor who was well-liked around the neighborhood for his calm and compassionate nature, who lived a fifteen-minute walk down the road with his three daughters (Amara, joined a few years later by Tiana and Trinity). Another sister, Maskia, who worked for an electric company, lived four hours away in a sweltering town called Ridgecrest with her daughter Diedre and sons Talib and Masego. Then there was another brother, Stephen, who throughout his life would half-heartedly dabble in politics and in prison; he was imprisoned after hijacking a plane to Cuba during the Black Power movement. Stephen's girlfriend left him after he couldn't keep a job, and he eventually became homeless. As far as I know, he sometimes lived with his son Robert and his two daughters.

There was also Joshua. I've met him just once, at a Christmas family reunion dinner held at my house in 2017. Uncle Joshua had also done time, condemned to a life sentence in prison after shooting at a police officer, though the officer hadn't been wounded. Within the last year, my uncle was released prematurely due to his age and illness. Then there was a brother named James, who molested my mother when she was five years old. It took her over twenty years to speak out about the horrific event, cradling that dark secret inside her like an unseen cancer, but it probably comes as no surprise that my siblings and I have never met this particular uncle. Rumor has it that he lives somewhere in Detroit. Truth is, I couldn't care less.

It was her brother Kahari and her sister Ledesi with whom my mother went to the movie theater on the night of March 29, 1980—my original due date. They took Derrick, Sanaa, Nala, and Amara with them, and watched *Kramer vs. Kramer,* a film that chronicles a couple's divorce and its impact on everyone involved, especially their kid. Ironic? Don't even get me started.

My mother was in labor during the movie, but she wasn't ready to go to the hospital, knowing from experience what the real cramps would feel like and when the timing would be right. Afterward, they took her to Farrell's Ice Cream Parlor, an old-school favorite with a 1950s vibe thanks to its checkered floor, player piano, flocked wallpaper, and brass ceiling tiles. She didn't eat much, knowing that labor is easier on an empty stomach. She did, however, spend as much of the night as she could with her family, also knowing that life is easier when you can lean on people who care about you.

...

I gasped my first breath around 2 a.m. on March 30, 1980, emerging in a hospital room under the care of a female doctor who predicted that I'd be a girl because my heartbeat had been so quick. After four hours of labor, my mother was rushed away so the doctors could remove a cyst. My father, despite his promise to be there for us, was late to the hospital. And thus my grandmother—a strong, sarcastic, big-hearted, chain-smoking, nurturing grandmother who'd likely blow off the head of any big bad wolf who messed with her—was the first to hold me, and most likely the first to love me.

So there I was: Constance Diedre Grays, my mother's fourth child.

Perhaps it's ironic that my father still got to name me. *Constance,* he insisted, because that was a queen's name, and I was his little princess. My mom selflessly gave me my middle name, Diedre, after one of my older cousins; that original Diedre was going through a lot, and my mom thought that it would make her happy to have someone named after her. (It did.) And Grays, because we were the Grays, which seems so very fitting when describing my childhood. It wasn't a matter of black and white. Life is never that straightforward. We lived in the liminal space of gray, a twilight zone where nothing seemed to change and yet where, strangely and simply, everything was possible.

In a world that could be so violent and bleak, there were so many pockets of sunshine and laughter. There were bedtime stories and sibling secrets and bike rides. There were barbeques at the beach and family holidays. There were books and movies and jazz. There were my parents dancing in the living room to the groove of Stevie Wonder's "All I Do." And there was me, finding my way, cooing at two months old. At eleven months, I'd taken my first steps, stumbling toward my beaming father as he held out a bowl of popcorn and said, "Come and get it."

I went, as oblivious as Hansel and Gretel trekking toward that gingerbread house in the heart of some dark European wood.

MY PROTECTOR

Growing up, I think I'd always sensed that Derrick was the He-Man to my Wonder Woman. My mother has told me that I used to bruise my butt in my attempt to follow him downstairs (lucky for me, when I had just learned to walk, we were living in an apartment with indoor stairs). I'd mastered walking *up* the stairs; walking *down* the stairs was another story. Derrick would often jump out of bed and rouse me awake. "Come on, Connie, let's watch cartoons!" he'd chortle, heading downstairs where we'd curl up on the carpet in front of the big old box. He would grab my hand and help me along down the steps.

One day, I decided that I was going down on my own. I bounced all the way down the stairs, my butt—cushioned by Pampers, the company that should have marketed itself as a baby-butt-armor brand—colliding against each step. From then on, it was our favorite morning ritual: the downward climb, the cheap generic cereal, and the adventures of He-Man,

ThunderCats, Inspector Gadget, and Wonder Woman…Due to our household dynamics, Derrick and I quickly learned to be self-sufficient.

Derrick, the third-eldest in our family, always had a mind of his own. When he was in first grade, my mother started taking him to the local community pool for swimming lessons. The problem? Derrick despised swimming. He'd come home at the end of each swimming session and declare that someone had stolen his swim trunks. My parents therefore kept buying him swim trunks. Eventually, they discovered that nobody had been stealing Derrick's trunks; he'd been throwing them into garbage bins. When my mother confronted him, his response was straightforward: "I don't like to swim."

Ah, the irony. Have you ever met a pool-loathing little guy from San Diego who grew up to join the Navy? That was my brother. I'm not sure exactly when Derrick gained a tolerance for water, but the transition happened at some point. I doubt that the "somebody stole my swim trunks" spiel would have worked as well on a commissioned Navy commander.

When Derrick was in second grade, his distaste for swimming was rivaled only by his distaste for the school bus. On a warm September day, my nine-month-pregnant mother walked Derrick to the bus stop, Michael and me in tow. During breakfast, through the apartment door, down the stairs, along the sidewalk, to the curb…Derrick grumbled all the way.

"I don't want to go…" he pouted.

My mom was adamant. "You have to."

"I don't want to go."

"You're going to miss the bus."

"I don't want to go!"

Within mere feet of the bus stop, Derrick tore his hand from our mother's and took off running, knowing that she could not run after him and catch him. When our mother finally made it home, we found Derrick waiting right inside the front door. He glanced at our mother's furious face and took a deep breath.

"I told you I didn't want to go and ride the bus," he explained solemnly.

But perhaps it was Derrick's stubbornness that gave him both spine and steel. When he was nine years old and I was seven, he and I became our family's official shoppers. Given my dad's absence and my relatives' busy lives, Mom would take the two of us everywhere with her; we were the responsible ones, who could help man the deck whenever our mom's life was threatening to capsize under the weight of too many kids running all around inside the lifeboat, which was practically always.

One afternoon, my mother loaded us all up in the car and took us to Food Basket on Faramont Avenue, our go-to grocery store. She parked, shooed us out of the car, and ushered us into the store, waddling behind us with a belly full of unborn Laila. At some point, she started to stumble between the aisles, clutching at some shelves to keep her balance.

"We can't shop today," she told Derrick, gesturing to the rest of us. "I don't feel so good. Come on, come on, let's go."

Once we all made it back to the car, Derrick tapped her shoulder. "Mom, what's your list? What do you want to buy? Give it to me."

Partly bemused, partly trying to keep her head from spinning, she handed him the list.

Derrick tore the sheet of paper in half and gave me one piece. "Me and Connie are going to go shopping," he announced. He glanced at me and I gave him a small smile, always proud to be included in whatever grand master plan my older brother was hatching. "We know where everything is."

Mom frowned. "No, I don't think so."

"Yes we are," he insisted, reaching over and pulling my hand. "Come on, Connie, we're gonna do this."

With my hand in Derrick's, I let him pull me out of the car and lead me back to the sliding front doors of Food Basket, my other hand clutching half a torn list, my feet carrying me away from a car full of bickering siblings and a heavily pregnant mother. Together, we entered the air-conditioned labyrinth of food and household goods, treading the familiar aisles and mentally checking things off the list until we met up again at the cash register. The cashier smiled at us endearingly and rang up all the items. We must have looked so tiny, stretching our arms from our baskets to the register, craning our heads to see the total cost. We paid the requested amount and headed back to the car, lugging the groceries with us.

"Twenty-two dollars and fourteen cents," Derrick announced, handing our mother the change and reciting a couple of items that hadn't been available in the store. She smiled at us gratefully.

And for the next four months till Laila was born and Mom could walk without waddling again, that's how we brought food to the table.

The Food Basket folks got used to their youngest regulars: a nine- and seven-year-old with two halves of a scribbled list, wandering through the aisles and loading up baskets. After a while, maybe it didn't seem so odd to see us two skinny kids navigating through the store. They even forgave me that one time when a huge glass bottle of Welch's Grape Juice slipped through my fingers and dropped to the floor with a resounding crash, flooding the floor of the aisle with purple juice and glass. My face flamed with shame and dread. I cringed at the shouting I was about to hear. Instead, the grocery clerks ran over to console me: "It happens" and "We'll clean it up, it's all right!" and "Are you okay? Did you hurt yourself?"

I'm never, ever, ever going shopping again! I thought to myself morosely, too embarrassed to do more than nod at them before scampering away.

Never didn't last very long. I didn't have the luxury of moving out of town or hiding under a rock for the rest of my life. Our dad was absent most of the time, a fact that began to stir a little fire of resentment deep in my belly—directed primarily at my father for his negligence, and partially at my mother for her doormat attitude. By the end of the week, Derrick and I were doing our usual rounds at Food Basket.

My fear of shopping began to ebb as my self-confidence grew. Walking along the aisles and picking up boxes and packages, I felt very adult. I liked feeling in control and independent. I wasn't a bread-winner yet, but I was a bread-buyer; my family needed me. I shouldered that responsibility with pride.

Our partnership wasn't limited to just grocery shopping. Wherever little Derrick went, littler Constance was sure to follow. He couldn't even escape me during the weekends. His best friend, Lucas, who lived in the same apartment complex, would show up outside our door on some Saturday mornings. He and Derrick would be ready to hang out with their friends, whether that meant going to the park or meandering in a store or just dawdling around the neighborhood.

"Mom, I'm going out to play with Lucas," Derrick would holler on his way out.

"I'm going too!" I'd announce bossily, bouncing up from the floor and discarding whatever toy I may have been playing with.

Derrick's smile would turn upside down with annoyance. "*No, you're not going.*"

"Yes, I am. Mommy! Aren't I going with Derrick?"

"No, we don't want her to come with us," Derrick would insist.

"Take your sister," our mother would say, and that would be the end of it.

That's how I found myself tagging along with Derrick and his friends one crisp Saturday morning, heading over to the local 7-Eleven. Filled with delicious snacks and arcade games, that place had practically become a mecca for the neighborhood kids. The boys quickly grouped around the video games and began pooling their coins, taking turns playing. I watched for a while until I got bored, then began to wander through the aisles.

A strange woman approached me in the store. "Oh!" she exclaimed, staring down at me and baring her teeth in a wide grin. Her lips were painted bright red, as if she'd just stained her mouth by eating beets—or blood. Her smile did not reach her eyes. "How are you doing? I haven't seen you in so long!"

I stopped in my tracks, confused. I didn't recognize her, but she spoke to me as if she knew me.

"Your grandmother would be so happy to see you!" She extended a hand in my direction, her fingers slender and well-manicured, and beckoned. "Come with me; let's go pay her a quick visit. Okay? Come on, let's go…"

I don't know you! I bolted away and raced toward my brother. "Derrick!" I gasped, half-crying. "There's a lady! She's trying to kidnap me! She's trying to take me somewhere!"

My brother snapped to attention at my agitation. "It's okay, Connie," he said. "Don't worry. I got you. Hide in here." He pushed me into the narrow space between the two video arcade machines. "Hurry!"

The boys resumed playing, keeping an eye on me and whirling around at random moments to ensure that no crazy lady was creeping up on us. I huddled in the space between them and hid, a little less scared, knowing that Derrick would never let a stranger steal me away.

The lady soon left the store. When the boys finished playing and we walked home, Derrick excitedly shared the story of my near-abduction. "Mom! This lady tried to take Connie! She tried to take her! But I took care of it…"

Derrick did take care of it. He took care of all of us. I could count on him to be there for me even when he didn't want to; he'd always make sure I was safe. Whenever it was in his power, he protected me and dragged me along with him so I wouldn't be by myself. He was a father figure who attempted to look out for me; in time, it would be Derrick who interrogated my first boyfriends. When Derrick tried out for football, I joined the cheerleading team.

To a huge extent, it was Derrick who showed me what I needed to do to survive in my family and helped me break free from my cocoon.

ALL SORTS OF SMILES

Sometime during childhood—likely as a result of the disillusionment I felt with my parents, and particularly my father—I concluded that the important thing isn't whether or not someone smiles at you. If they do smile at you, it's the type of smile that counts. And there are many types of smiles.

There's the polite smile, for instance. This is the smile that Aunt Ledesi sometimes wore when she saw someone doing something that she didn't like but she didn't feel that it was appropriate to say something. This was the sort of smile that people sometimes gave each other in the grocery store, or when walking down the street, or at church. It was the bland, polite, *I'm smiling because I've got to be smiling* type of smile.

There's the fake smile too, which is worse than the polite smile because you know that the person isn't even trying. At worst, they don't have good intentions. At best, they just don't care enough to mean it.

Then there's the real smile, the sort of smile that reaches the eyes and crinkles the skin and gives that person a sparkle. The smile that exudes sunbeams and happy vibes. The smile that automatically makes your own lips curl upward in return as if your face becomes a reflection. Uncle Kahari and my cousin Amara were adored within our family for their real smiles and all the real compassion that came with them, but I met some other such smilers in my early years too. These people exuded values and traits that resonated with me, however subconsciously, and they helped to create a set of standards in my heart that I would uphold more solidly many years later.

Chris Daniels was one of the most memorable examples. My memory of Chris is of a slim white woman with a sweet face and glasses. Her brown hair was thick and wavy with rich, honey-hued undertones that seemed to match the soft, honeyed warmth of her voice. She worked in the nursery of the local clinic, Kaiser Permanente, and she smelled of babies. She was our family's child practitioner for years, taking care of me (and all my female siblings) from infancy until I was twelve years old. She was kind to all of us, and she even gave Mom her private office number. Anytime one of us needed any appointment, she would get us in the same day.

Happily married and the mother of two girls, Chris Daniels seemed all I could ever hope to be: independent, hard-working, smart, strong, and happy.

She always greeted me with a smile and focused all of her attention on me, making me feel as important and as special as the president of the United States. "Hi, Connie," she'd say, welcoming me into the brightly lit examination room. "How are you today?"

One time I remember I entered the clinic for a regular check-up, clutching my baby doll with me. It seems ironic now that I'd be lugging around a baby, as if I hadn't had my fill of them; there were plenty of real-life ones squalling at home and having constant parties in their diapers. But I'd always liked babies, so I cherished my doll.

"I see your baby there," Chris said, smiling at the doll as if the doll could smile back. "What's her name?"

I hugged my baby doll close to me for a moment before plucking up my courage and turning her plastic face toward the nurse practitioner. "Katie!"

"That's a beautiful name." Chris smiled. We talked about my siblings, about the health of my mother's latest baby—it seemed there was always a "latest baby" around—and about school. "Are you enjoying it?" she asked me.

Most adults asked questions and did not wait for a response. It was like they asked things just to go through the motions, because they *had* to, just like they smiled at each other because they *had* to. But Chris never asked rhetorical questions. I realized that the woman was waiting for an answer. I nodded my head.

She shone a light into my eyes. I tried not to blink. "What is your favorite subject?"

"English." *Duh,* I added cheerfully in my head.

"Who is your favorite teacher?"

"Mr. D," I said immediately. He was my teacher at the time—first grade. I knew that I had a long way to go before I finished school and I would have many more teachers over the years, but I was convinced that Mr. D would always be my favorite. I liked him better even than my kindergarten teacher, who had always given my mom books to read to me and who'd often praised me for staying within the lines while coloring.

The irony is that we never even called Mr. D by his full last name: *Mr. Delgado.* He asked us all to call him "Mr. D," knowing it was easier, and so that name stuck. He was a mustached Mexican man, thin and brown-haired and of average height, somewhere in his early thirties. He had a love for banana, peanut butter, and cheese sandwiches that made my stomach turn, and he had a dream—inspired by a love of all things sci-fi—of someday living in an underwater kingdom. His love for kids was genuine; you could tell by his quiet voice, friendly except when it needed to be firm; you could tell by his casual outfits, humble and never overdressed; you could tell by his smile, the type that reached his eyes.

I loved Mr. D because he seemed to exemplify for me all that a real man could and should be. He spent time speaking with students and getting to know each of us on an individual level, listening attentively and remembering what we told him. He had no kids of his own, as far as I knew, although he was married; perhaps *we* were his kids, in his mind. Best of all, Mr. D was encouraging and appreciative—more than anyone else I'd ever met. He told me what a good student I was, and this paved the way for a future in which I was determined to strive to be a straight-A student. He appreciated me for being myself, not for who I was helping or for what chore I'd taken on so that my mom wouldn't have to. He supported *my* future. He made me feel like I mattered, and believed in me before I believed in myself.

Sometime during the school year, Mr. D asked my mother if he could give me a job. He would often tell me that I was his favorite student, and he wanted to help me. So, with my mom's permission, I started grading papers for five dollars a week. It was my first earned cash, and I felt like a million bucks every time I received my salary. I felt capable, independent, and successful.

As much as I loved Mr. D, though, it was Chris Daniels' job that I admired more. My focus returned to her as she finished examining my ears, and she nodded approvingly. "Say *aaaah*," she said, holding what looked like a popsicle stick.

"I want to be like you when I grow up," I said.

"That's wonderful, Connie." Her small, absent smile expanded automatically into a huge grin and she met my gaze for a moment. "You can be whatever you want."

The check-up did not last long enough. Too soon, it was time to go. "Can I have diapers for my baby?" I asked Chris as she helped me off the examination table.

As usual, she didn't just give me diapers. She gave me a blanket for my baby, a bag, bottles, and a real-life old stethoscope that probably didn't work so well anymore but looked absolutely amazing.

Soon after, my mom began going to a different doctor's office that had opened up closer to home. Then she showed up at Kaiser one time to deliver Jeremiah. Chris Daniels, doing her rounds, saw that a baby had been born with the last name "Grays." She showed up at my mom's room and surprised her.

"Evonne!" Chris beamed as she walked in and greeted my mother. "I saw a baby with the name *Grays* and I said to myself, this has to be Evonne. I knew it was you."

My mother greeted her joyfully, albeit a bit embarrassed.

"I knew he was yours, but I had to come see for myself. You have a beautiful baby!" Chris cooed and fussed over tiny baby Jeremiah, welcoming him sweetly into a harsh world. "Where have you been, Evonne?"

"I've been hiding out," my mother admitted.

Before Chris left the hospital, she bought a card and a lovely plant for my mother. It wasn't the last we'd see of her; she was my practitioner until I was twelve years old, yet she was so much more to me, this woman who showed me what women were capable of, who opened my eyes to a world where I could dream and where the possibilities of becoming whatever I wanted were endless, who had the sort of smile that reached the eyes and creased the skin and filled her with an inner light.

It's not the skin or eye or hair color that matters in a person, nor their height or their weight or their gender. It's the smile that makes the man—or woman. Remember that there are all sorts of smiles.

6

LITTLE WONDER WOMAN

A week before Christmas in 1985, a little kinky-haired Wonder Woman broke her arm. It burned fiercer than the Lasso of Truth, which hadn't been tied quite so well around the bedpost. This event isn't something you'll ever read about in a DC comic book or see in a Hollywood film. It was a private matter. It happened in my home, in front of my brothers.

Oh, wait. You and my five-year-old self haven't been introduced; at the time, I also went by the alias *Wonder Woman.*

I'd been racing around the bedroom, my cape swirling, swinging my Lasso of Truth, and imploring my two little brothers to pay attention. I tied the jump rope on one end of the bed and then scrambled up to the top of the bunkbed, where I tied the other end to the upper bedpost. I grinned and prepared to slide across the gap.

"Watch me!" I called to them.

"I wanna see!" Jeremiah exclaimed. "Can you do it?"

"Of course I can! I'm Wonder Woman! Watch, watch!"

"Big deal." Michael was more skeptical. "Watch what? Watchu gonna do?"

"I'm gonna fly!" I told him. "From here to there! You just watch!"

Wonder Woman was all I could ever aspire to be. She was a female badass: strong, courageous, big-hearted, and authentic. She could fend for herself and didn't need a man to take care of her, having spent her adolescence training her body and mind on an island of warrior women.

A moment later, I found myself on the ground, fallen at the foot of the bunkbed with my arm having cracked against the wood. The jump rope had come undone when I tried to catapult from the top of the bunkbed to the top of the opposite bed. The broken bone burned and throbbed; pain lanced through my entire body. It was intensified by any and all movement. I screamed. Tears burst from my eyes and rolled down my cheeks, two tiny rivers that I was helpless to stop—that I didn't *want* to stop, because I needed a release.

Michael gaped at me, realizing something was wrong but not knowing how to respond. Jeremiah's face crumpled; his dimples and smile vanished as he cried along with me, either in vocal support or in disappointment. This wasn't the show that they'd been promised. Wonder Woman wasn't pulling some amazing stunt. Instead, they got Wonder Woman screaming until her parents came sprinting into the room.

My father reached me first, his eyes wide and frightened. He grabbed my arm and wobbled it as if to get the blood circulating, trying to shake out the pain, trying to convince me that I was fine. "Don't worry, Connie, it's nothing," he consoled me, oblivious to the fact that he couldn't have tortured me more if he'd tried. "You'll be all right. It's okay!"

I screamed louder, tears blurring my vision, and tried to pull away. The knotted sleeves of my sweater came loose, slipping from where they'd been tied around my shoulders. I unclenched my other fist and dropped the end of the jump rope.

"No, no, it's not okay!" my mom exclaimed. "There's something wrong!"

"She's fine," my dad insisted, drawing on absolutely zero medical expertise. He tapped my arm the way doctors tap on kids' knees with their little hammers, as if his good intentions and clumsy torture-treatment would magically set my bone back in place. "She just hurt herself a little."

"Can't you see you're hurting her?" My mom placed herself between us, her voice sharp and her hair frazzled and fighting to break free from its hair-tie. She pushed his hands away and bent down to inspect my arm. "This is a different type of crying—I know my daughter!"

"Evonne, she just fell over."

"I'm taking her to the hospital!"

Wonder Woman was lucky to have her mother home with her that day. My mom called my grandmother, who was driven over by Jim. Jim took one look at my screaming face and seemed ready to hightail it away just to escape the noise. He didn't though, partially because he realized the pain was real and partially perhaps nailed in place by my grandmother's steely eyes. Though he was my grandmother's second ex-husband, I'd always thought of him as her tall, balding, mustached, private chauffeur. They lived in an apartment complex farther away from us—on the same floor, with their doors across the hall from each other; though divorced, Jim still loved my grandmother, and he drove her around after she was unable to drive herself any longer. Though withdrawn at times and not the most animated of conversationalists, he loved all of us, in his own quiet way. He drove us all to the hospital that day, waiting while my grandmother and mother rushed me inside.

When I came home with the cast hours later, my dad's face fell in shame once he saw me. "Oh, Connie-coo!" he said. "Oh no…I'm so sorry. I didn't know…"

I brushed past him, ignoring his apologies.

"How do you feel?"

I didn't reply.

"Your cast will be off soon," he attempted again. "It'll just be a few weeks..."

Yes, my siblings and friends would soon be clamoring to sign my cast. Yes, I'd be an exciting center of attention for the next few days before my family lost interest and the chores piled up again. Yes, this would remain as one of my most memorable Christmas seasons. And yes, it wasn't my father's fault that I fell from the bed and broke my arm. But he'd added to my pain, out of pure ignorance and irresponsibility, while diminishing its importance.

I gazed at him with all the solemnity and righteousness of a pained five-year-old. I think I had begun realizing, even then, that I was already outgrowing my father.

...

Uncle Kahari took us everywhere my father couldn't or wouldn't: the movies, the zoo, the new diner downtown, Disneyland, the circus, the beach, and basically anywhere that a family would crave to go. Every couple of years, we would do family reunions. Considering the scope of my family, those could get huge. This didn't faze Uncle Kahari, of course. He'd hire a huge van (or two, when needed) to load us all up; he'd coordinate the itinerary, the food we needed, and the when and where of the stops along the way; he'd pay for it all, knowing that the rest of us couldn't really afford to chip in. I didn't realize the extent of his generosity and sacrifice until decades later.

During smaller family excursions and given that we only had one car (my mother's) at the time, Uncle Kahari would make multiple trips back and forth from the apartment complex to whatever our destination was, ensuring that all of the relatives could enjoy the outing together. My siblings and I would pile up in the car when it was our turn to be driven somewhere, never guessing that Uncle Kahari and Aunt Ledesi had already been to sandy La Jolla Shores or lovely Mission Bay Beach at 5 a.m. that day so that Aunt Ledesi could hold a spot for all of us. Then

Uncle Kahari would go back and forth, piling up people and toys and barbeque equipment and food and extra clothing and whatever else was necessary. He did it for years without complaint and without fanfare, because that's just the kind of man he was.

His compassion and reliability were, as usual, put to the test one summer's day in San Diego's most famous park.

The day began peacefully enough. I was enjoying an unusual excursion with my mother and a couple of my siblings, spending the sunny morning in the gorgeous 1,200-acre urban cultural park that's been around since 1835. We loved Balboa Park for its immense grassy lawns, its gardens and walking paths, its many museums and theaters, and the San Diego Zoo. But like all the beautiful and touristy destinations of the world, Balboa Park was not without its shady characters; as it was in the heart of downtown San Diego, a good number of drug addicts and homeless folks could be found prowling through the park.

I'm not sure when she realized her purse was missing. One moment, we were rolling around and playing in the grass, my mother watching us from her bench; the next, we heard her shouting, "My purse!" and turned to see her on her feet, frantically scouting around the bench, desperately hoping that her purse had just fallen somehow or had maybe sprouted wings and floated over to a nearby tree branch and hadn't been taken from her when she'd looked the other way.

"Get over here," she gestured at us. Her face had lost its serene expression. Her eyes were wide under her furrowed brow, and her mouth was a thin red line. "Come on, we've got to find a phone!" She started rummaging through her pockets. "Who has a quarter? Connie, you got a quarter?"

"I don't have a quarter." I panicked, infected by her desperation. "Mommy, why did you leave your purse like that? How could you? How are we gonna get home? Where's your money? All your stuff is in there!"

"Maybe the car keys fell out somewhere," my mother said, hopeful and desperate. "Help me look for the keys! They'll turn up somewhere!"

I did. They didn't.

Uncle Kahari came as fast as he could after my mother's call. He took one look at my mother's teary face and bit back his automatic reaction to lecture her.

"How could I be so dumb?" she mourned. "What do I do now?"

"It's okay, Kay-Kay." Uncle Kahari soothed her with a quick hug and his quiet voice, the sort of low and gentle voice that soothes wild horses and douses arguments quickly. "We'll take care of this. Tell me exactly what happened."

Wiping at her tears, she told him about how her purse was stolen, practically from under her nose, probably when she'd stood up to go throw something in the garbage bin just a few steps away.

"How long ago did it happen?" he asked. "What was in your purse?"

When she mentioned her wallet and her keys, Uncle Kahari immediately called a locksmith. "Don't worry," he told her as we all walked to the parking lot of the park and waited together. "These things happen."

He paid the man for the new key, filled my mom's car with gas, and gave her whatever extra cash he had on him. No complaints, no lectures, no fuss—and the *no lectures* was especially surprising because Uncle Kahari was a professor to the bone; he never passed up an opportunity to lecture. If he did, we suspected him of running a fever or something. (For my mom's sake, and for the same reason, I'm glad Derrick wasn't with us that day; mature as a hundred-year-old oak tree, my older brother's lectures and disappointment level would have topped even Uncle Kahari's.)

Uncle Kahari didn't let my mom pay him back. When she insisted, he just squeezed her shoulder. "It's okay, sis," he said. "Just make sure the next time you go out to do something, you don't leave your purse unattended." His wink softened the jab of the lecture. "You just might wanna keep it with you."

They say that most families are like chocolate—sweet, with a few nuts. Our family certainly had its share of strange and unlikeable characters, at least in my eyes, but it just as surely included incredible individuals who were compassionate and brave enough to step in when key protagonists such as my father stepped out. Yes, there was a sense of familial obligation. Yes, blood ran thicker than water. But that doesn't always matter, does it? It doesn't mean that family members automatically step in and provide a helping hand. It's always a choice.

You can't force someone to stay. You can't force someone to love you.

7

STAGNATION

It was the summer of 1986, a month or two after my father had shown up drunk at our home and I had refused to open the door, and the nation had been busy making progress. Martin Luther King Jr. Day was observed for the first time that year, NASA launched the *Columbia* space shuttle, the U.S. Senate outlawed genocide, *Out of Africa* won an Oscar for Best Picture, and 6.5 million people formed a human chain from NYC to California to raise money against hunger and homelessness.

But in my world, things hadn't changed. Daddy had been drinking again. His demons were having a kickboxing match inside his body; he stumbled occasionally as he walked, as if one of them had punched him too hard from the inside. He and Mommy spent too much time screaming at each other. I don't remember why now, but the reasons feel endless. I would often cry during and after their fights, feeling afraid and helpless to do anything, my toys and books and laughter all forgotten.

One evening, my parents had begun their usual shouting match. I heard my father yell the all-too-familiar ultimatum: "I'm leaving!" He grabbed my mother's car keys from the kitchen counter and began to walk toward the front door.

"No!" she shrilled at him. "You're not taking my car!"

He pushed her roughly away as she attempted to wrestle the keys from his hand. Mommy was caught off guard for a moment, but she caught herself in time, one hand protectively over her belly. She was pregnant again, and visibly so, but my father didn't spare her a second glance. I watched as he stormed out of our second-story apartment, out the front door, and into the hot Californian afternoon, down the rickety white steps and along the sidewalk toward the parking lot. My mother ran after him. I ran after my mother.

I remember how the light of the setting sun caught in my mother's curly hair and seemed to set it afire. I remember the clacking of my brother's marbles as he and his friends played on the lawn that flanked the parking lot and appeared as a patch of green between our apartment building and the next complex. I remember the pounding of my six-year-old heart as I followed my parents down the steps and froze at the bottom, clinging to the pale blue railing until my fingers hurt.

They chose that parking lot, half asphalt and half cement, with its painted white lines and its cracked cement, for their battlefield.

My father managed to get into the car before my mother reached him. He locked the doors and rolled up the windows. Mommy started beating her fists against the glass that separated his face from hers. "No!" she yelled. "Get out of my car! Give me my keys! You're not taking my car!"

The neighbors had heard us by now; heads were poking out of doors and windows. It was drama in the Grays District as usual. But things hadn't gotten too crazy yet. No one had interfered.

"Move out the way," he yelled back at her, his voice slightly muffled by the glass. "Move out the way!"

"No! I'm not moving! Get out of my damn car!"

"Move out the way!"

"I'm not moving! You dumb drunk, this is my car! You're not taking my car!"

After a bit more of my mom's incessant yelling and banging, my father'd had enough. It was like a green light went off in his drunken state, a light that signified something along the lines of *screw this, I'm out.* He started the engine, switched gears, shifted the car, and moved it forward to drive away, hitting my mom in the process.

He hit her hard enough to floor her, knocking her off her feet. I screamed; my brother screamed. My mother lay in the parking lot, stunned, and watched my father drive away with the family's only car—her car.

You can't force someone to stay.

My fourteen-year-old brother Andre burst out of the house and ran to our mother as I and eight-year-old Derrick looked on, dumbfounded. "Mom! Are you okay?" He was crying. "Are you okay?"

"I'm all right." Tears spilled down my mother's cheeks as she let Andre help her up. "Don't worry."

I didn't spare a second thought for my dad right then. I was glad he was gone. I didn't want him back, spreading anger and hurt throughout the neighborhood.

Someone shouted. I looked up to see my Aunt Ledesi burst out from her downstairs apartment and rush toward us. "Kay!" she cried. "Kay, are you all right? Kay, what the hell happened? You should call the police on him! He hit you with a car, how could he do that?" She steadied my mom, wiping away her tears with her hands as if my thirty-year-old mother was one of the first-graders Aunt Ledesi tended to as a teacher's assistant. Aunt Ledesi was actually a year younger than my mom, but her stern, clipped voice carried authority and didn't have time for nonsense. "He stole your car! He can't do this to you, Kay! You just need to make him stop doing this to you, you can't keep letting him back over and over again—it always ends like this! He could've killed you!" Aunt Ledesi shook her head in despair. Rage hardened her voice and her eyes. "What were you thinking?"

It would be many years before I'd fully realize how much my mother's relatives had to work to support our family. Every time my dad attacked or abandoned us, they were the ones who had to step in and try to fill his place. This obligation frustrated and saddened them, and strained our relationship with them. They were just as poor and had their own share of hardships; shouldering our cross should not have been their burden to carry. Mommy couldn't break away, though. Each time Daddy returned crying and apologizing, she took him back and then they brought yet another child or two or three into the world. Before my eighteenth birthday, my parents had married and divorced each other three times, and I was the fourth of nine siblings.

My father was almost always missing—emotionally if not physically, especially once I grew up enough to understand what absence meant. My mother was almost always pregnant and depressed, but she didn't have the luxury of wallowing in her misery. There wasn't any time for that. She worked full-time, sometimes took on a second job, ran a household, and attempted to raise her kids. When my father would leave, she'd have her own tantrums and would threaten to run away and leave us alone. Perhaps she never meant it, because she never did leave, but those shrieks continue to haunt me. She followed her heart—that same traitorous, golden heart that made her always forgive my father—and stuck it out with us, a broken child raising lonely children.

"I'm sorry," my mom mumbled. She let my aunt herd us back toward the apartment complex. Around us, the world continued its progress, oblivious to our own stagnation. Later that summer, earthquakes would rattle the homes and hearts of southeastern Californians, rearranging pieces of the Earth in their attempt to fix it. President Reagan and Soviet leader Mikhail Gorbachev would meet in Iceland in a futile effort to end the Cold War and bring on peace. Mike Tyson, throwing punches like a trigger, would win his first world boxing title in November. By

December, the nation's unemployment rate would drop to 6.6 percent, the lowest it had been for the past six years.

Progress.

Meanwhile, there I was, cooking spaghetti on the stove as my mom fought to make ends meet with a handful of kids and a missing car. My father came back after a few days of zero contact. He returned the car to my mother, full of apologies and empty promises. She forgave him, of course.

I didn't.

8

THE GREATEST SHOW
ON EARTH

Life rolled on. The routine of my typical day depended on what trimester my mom found herself in. During the last three or four months of each pregnancy, she wasn't as physically fast or flexible. A lot of the work—from household chores to changing diapers to babysitting my siblings to outdoor errands—fell on my shoulders. Looking back today, she says that I was a bossy, independent, serious, and logical child. I'd always sensed that the majority of her attention and affection was reserved for the kids who "needed" her. Isn't that how it always goes? The squeaky wheel gets the grease.

The squeaky wheel, however, doesn't get to go to the circus.

One weekend morning in the summer of 1987, someone came knocking on our front door. It had dawned bright and sunny. I'd just finished my breakfast and had perched in front of the television to watch cartoons. At the sound of the knock, my breath caught in my seven-year-old throat; everyone in the apartment froze, wondering if our father had returned from his weeks-long stint of absence. Last night, one night in a string of other such nights, my brother Derrick had turned to our mother at seven o'clock and had announced, "It's seven; he's not coming" in a tragically matter-of-fact voice, reminding us that another day had gone by without our father around and that it was time to have dinner as a fatherless family.

My mother bravely strode to the door and cracked it open. Uncle Kahari beamed back at her, his daughter Amara half-hidden behind his leg and smiling at me shyly.

"Good morning, Kay!" he said cheerily, as usual calling her by her African name of choice, *Kay-Chinka*, which she'd chosen during the Black Power movement. No one within the family really used her original name after that, just like nobody really called my other relatives by their actual names anymore. Uncle Kahari glanced around the room until he saw me and winked. "Is Miss Connie here? I'm taking Amara to the circus and she refuses to go anywhere without her favorite partner-in-crime."

I gazed at him, wide-eyed. The circus? I was invited to the circus? I didn't know what the heck a circus was at the time, but it sure sounded wonderful if my cheery uncle and favorite cousin showed up at the door to whisk me away.

My mom never found it easy to refuse Uncle Kahari anything. She turned her head to look at me. "You want to go to the circus, Connie?"

As if I'd say no! I jumped to my feet and grinned until I thought my lips would split my face, running across the room to my uncle and cousin.

"That would be a yes," Uncle Kahari chuckled.

"Well, get dressed." My mom tilted her head toward the bedroom that I shared with all my siblings. "Can't go to the circus in your pajamas."

I bolted to the bedroom, my mother following more slowly. She watched me pick out my favorite outfit—a white short-sleeved shirt and plum-colored shorts patterned with a white stripe on the side. Ever the coordinator, I matched these with white socks and white shoes. I brushed my teeth and let my mother gather my hair into a ponytail. Then, unable to wait a moment longer, I ran back to the front door where my uncle and cousin were waiting for me.

And off we went!

The circus took my breath away. When we arrived outside, Uncle Kahari took our hands in his so we wouldn't get lost in the jostle of people. I clasped his hand tightly with my far-smaller fingers, feeling safe in his grip like a boat tethered to the port. The amount and diversity of people around me felt overwhelming, but it was nothing like what was waiting for me inside. We passed the ticket booth, where Uncle Kahari paid and handed each of us our beautiful tickets.

Ringling Bros and Barnum & Bailey Circus—The Greatest Show on Earth!

I felt that I could lose myself forever in that other world within the tents, a world colored like licorice and smelling of deliciously buttered popcorn, home to all manner of man and beast. There were so many sights and acts and things to see and do, so much energy and vibrancy pulsing from each stage, each tethered animal, and each colorfully painted acrobat's face. There were massive elephants with ears like enormous gray lily pads and trunks thicker than my arm. There were beautiful horses with long, sleek manes and proudly tapping hooves. Children grabbed fistfuls of confetti and threw it into the air so that festively colored pieces drifted around us like paper butterflies.

Amara and I sat together, sharing a huge bag of scrumptious popcorn, licking our fingertips after nearly every handful. Two years older than me, Amara was the type of girl who seemed always ready to bestow a gentle smile or a kind word. Whenever she visited, she would always promptly wash her hands and excitedly ask: "Can I hold the new baby?" Amara sometimes helped me with babysitting, feeding, and diaper changing. Her parents had divorced not long after she was born, and she lived with her father now as an only child with only one responsibility: to be her own best self. I envied her that.

But we were all of us lucky to have Uncle Kahari in our lives. Though there were few things he enjoyed more than having a beautiful woman by his side, he was a dependable father and an upstanding uncle. He took care of Amara and, perhaps feeding off of his example, she took care of me. Like my uncle, she dressed elegantly, spoke eloquently, loved generously, and smiled genuinely. I think she sensed how much I looked up to her and adored her; she always made room for me in her life, letting me feel included and important.

We cheered on the acrobats, oohing and aahing along with the crowd as the lithe men and women defied gravity and mortality and catapulted themselves from post to post. Amara gasped and pointed at the man on stilts, nearly as tall as an apartment building. I cringed at the clown, someone who could be anyone, hiding behind a thick mask of makeup.

And there were tigers and lions, roaring at me to tell me that the world was a very vast and exotic place, and I was just a speck in the midst of it all. I wanted to go where they'd come from. I wanted to travel as they did. There was a great big world that stretched far, far beyond the cramped two-bedroom apartment that I shared with my family.

In a way, I felt that the circus spoke to me. It wasn't in a language you'd hear with your ears. It wasn't even a dialogue that I could tangibly translate at the time. But I know what I heard.

You can reach incredible heights, the acrobats told me with every practiced swing of their limbs, *as long as you have the perseverance and the courage and the will.*

You can break through the mold, the dwarves and the men on stilts said, and it was spoken with the fact of their mere presence as they paraded across the stage, *and you will find your unique way, no matter how big or small you are or feel like.*

You can walk through fire, the tigers informed me with each snarl of determination as they leapt through blazing hoops, *and the fire will harden and strengthen you, and you will emerge through to the other side with all the beauty of a resurrected phoenix.*

I didn't know what sort of heights I would reach in my life. I had no idea what distance I could ever hope to cover. I had no idea, at the time, that I *would* have to walk through fire and make it out alive. But I sensed that there was more to life than what I'd tasted so far, and the circus opened my eyes to a new horizon of possibilities. I wanted to be more. I wanted to be free to *be*. The buzzing energy of the circus tapped into a deep-set and fierce yearning, a feeling that tugged at my heartstrings, though it took me years to label it.

A butterfly, nestled deep in the cocoon of my heart, was stirring into wakefulness.

PART 2
1988—1998

"WHATEVER YOU FEAR MOST HAS NO POWER—IT IS YOUR FEAR THAT
HAS THE POWER. THE THING ITSELF CANNOT TOUCH YOU. BUT IF YOU
ALLOW YOUR FEAR TO SEEP INTO YOUR MIND AND OVERTAKE YOUR
THOUGHTS, IT WILL ROB YOU OF YOUR LIFE."

—OPRAH WINFREY

9

A Way Out

One August afternoon when I was fourteen years old, I grabbed a bottle of aspirin and locked myself in the bathroom. My sisters and mother didn't notice, and Derrick wasn't home. I took a moment to gaze at myself for the last time in a toothpaste-speckled mirror.

Huge brown eyes stared back at me from a solemn face. Gone was the smile, gone was the sparkle. I saw pudgy cheeks on a face that hadn't quite lost its baby fat, framed by close-cropped bangs. I'd cut my hair earlier that year in an attempt to look like a member of TLC; instead, I ended up looking more like a boy. I stared at a forlorn teenager dressed in a black T-shirt, black shorts, and a blue vest.

Black and blue. It was a sensible combination. Those were the colors of my bruised heart.

I couldn't imagine spending one more minute in this house, this skin, this life. I'd grown up crammed in a tiny home with seven people.

For as long as I could remember, this family had included Mia, our schizophrenic sister who heard voices, helplessly spat out insults at us one moment and spoke kindly to us the next, and would someday spend time in prison for repeatedly stabbing her best friend during a mental breakdown (fortunately, the friend survived). It also included an older brother, Andre, who refused to move out or get a job and who bullied the rest of us incessantly. It also included Jeremiah, Michael, and Xavier, who had now been sent to live for six months with our father, who apparently was trying to prove himself a functional parent. In my younger brothers' place, however, and during another months-long stint when my father was *not* being a functional parent, we had temporarily housed my father's perverted younger brother, Cricket.

While my dad was gone, my mom got a job as the apartment manager in the neighborhood and we were able to move from a two-bedroom to a three-bedroom house further down the hill. My family was finally stable: we weren't on assistance anymore, I attended a school I liked, I was babysitting for other people and making some money, and my siblings and I didn't have to worry about our parents fighting. I could recall some good times with my dad, but those happy memories were always overshadowed by the wreckage and pain he left every time he abandoned us.

Then my mother informed us one day—casually, as if mentioning a forecast of rainfall—that she and my father would be getting back together.

No one asked us kids what we thought about that. Nobody said, "Hey, Connie? What do you think about an alcoholic, abusive, absent father coming back around for the third time after years of being M.I.A. and giving this whole 'family thing' another go?" It wasn't even a rhetorical question. It was a fact. He was coming back.

I knew he was *bad* for us. He was a liar, a thief, an abuser, and an addict. This was a man who'd been hit by cars several times when he was drunk, once so badly that he had to be airlifted to a hospital. I was five years old at the time and my parents were separated; nonetheless, my mom took him home and nursed him back to health. He stayed until he had healed and no longer looked like the Elephant Man. Then, no longer needing her, he high-tailed it back to L.A.

He was never going to change. My mother still didn't get it, and I doubted she ever would. The cycle would just repeat itself. Our household would again include—and, even more importantly, would be *directed by*—my father.

We'd be moving. I'd be forced into a new school, leaving behind my friends and my teachers and any semblance of being able to control my life. Dad wasn't coming back to open the lid on the little glass jar we called "life as we know it" and free us. No, that would be too straightforward, too optimistic. He was coming to smash the jar and cram us into another jar on the other side of town.

He was the last straw.

I couldn't handle sleeping with my mother, Mia, and my two younger sisters all in the same bed every night. I couldn't handle knowing that I was a pawn on life's shaky chessboard that my father could upend whenever he damn well pleased, every time it seemed like the rest of the family had just regained its footing. Every night, I cried myself to sleep. Every night, my mother ignored it. I felt lost, a dark-winged moth exhausted from circling around the lamp bulb of the sun for fourteen years.

I couldn't handle being invisible.

So the pills were looking pretty good right then. If I were Alice in Wonderland, these pills would have been inscribed with *Eat Me*. And there would have been subtext, too: *Free Yourself.*

I was terrified. But this was a way out. *Out* was the direction I sought. If you looked back on the road we'd traveled thus far, it seemed like my family had been following a crooked path for a very long time. It was as if we had a broken compass etched in our bones, and it seemed to always be pointing to a destination called *Trouble*.

TRAPPED LIKE A TREE

Perhaps the most unfair aspect of my parents' relationship was the contradictory nature of how they seemed to define their relationship to each other and to their children. My father was a cloud, floating over the land and materializing in the neighborhood whenever he felt like it. My mother was a tree, rooted to the ground and trapped.

Leaving was in my father's DNA. You'd think my mother, seven years his senior, would have been used to it. You'd think that his behavior would have hardened her heart against him. Each time he left, it was as if he took a piece of her with him, until there were only slivers left of the person she was before meeting him. I was very young when I first saw my mother shatter. I remember how she crumpled to the floor in the middle of our apartment, overcome with anguish, and just cried and cried.

"What a mess," she groaned and wept. She hugged herself as sobs racked her body. "I'm all alone. I'm all alone! What am I gonna do with all these kids alone?"

All of us gathered around her, hugging her and patting her on the back. Her sudden and absolute distress engulfed us, instinctively making us fear for and pity her. "It's okay, Mommy," we said, attempting to echo soothing words that she often told us. That only made her cry harder.

It may be one of my earliest memories, and certainly one of the most traumatic. We kids were all my mother really had, and all we had was each other. We defined her life as much as she defined our childhood. We were both her cross and her sunlight. Now, decades later, whenever we rummage together through boxes brimming with old photographs, my mother looks at them and says, "This is my life. All I had was you kids."

Looking back now, I can see this was true.

Evonne Grays was human. She had her spurts of selfishness and self-pity, but her intentions were good and her heart was untainted. Even though she could not make the time or energy to express her love to us to the degree that we needed it, she tried—and she certainly could have used all the help she could get. Unfortunately, teenagers tend to have minds of their own; they can sometimes be selfish, rude, or unkind without realizing the full extent of their actions. I remember an instance that involved Derrick, which happened when I was eleven years old. Derrick was thirteen at the time. He came home from school that day and found my younger siblings and I watching something on TV. He grabbed the remote and changed the channel. We promptly complained to my mother, who ordered him to change it back.

"No," Derrick retorted. "They dunno what they're watching anyway."

"Move," our mother said firmly. She grabbed the remote and shoved him out of the way when he wouldn't budge. "Go to your room."

He folded his arms across his chest and refused to move.

"Move!" she repeated angrily.

The rest of us watched in awe as the scene played out. Our mother's wet eyes indicated that she hated what she was forced to do, but her steely voice and manner indicated that she knew it was necessary. It was a showdown; in our father's absence, she had to exhibit dominance. She was the boss and she had to be respected. Despite how little she was and despite how tall Derrick was, our mother used every ounce of strength and pushed him all the way to the bedroom. She pushed so she would not be seen as a pushover. She closed the door on Derrick once he was inside, and held the knob for what seemed like an eternity. Finally he gave up trying to come out. Then she closed herself up in her own bedroom, crying and praying, grappling with her need to discipline a disrespectful son, her disappointment in his reaction, and her bitterness at the fact that she was raising nine kids practically by herself.

Derrick avoided us all night. Our mom brought him dinner to his bedroom anyway, following that big heart of hers—pumping with compassion, love, and forgiveness—that so many people in her life had crushed or had taken for granted. The next morning, after getting dressed and ready for school, Derrick left his bedroom and knocked on our mom's bedroom door. She opened the door immediately.

"I'm sorry," he said.

Our mother opened her arms and embraced him. "You are the example, Derrick," I heard her say. "You have to do the right thing. You have to be fair and not be disrespectful. I need your help…do the right thing because it's the right thing to do."

It was instances like that which made me *want* to shoulder some of the weight and the responsibilities. Our mother had a good heart, even if I grew to mistrust her judgment and resent her tantrums. Just by sticking around and struggling to support us—a complete juxtaposition to our father's behavior—she proved that she cared. Her skirmish with Derrick reminded me that she was the head of the house and had to be respected as such. It also warmed my heart to realize that Derrick took after her; he couldn't hold a grudge for long. Despite his own hurts and wants, he always made the choice to put the family first.

At least for as long as he could take it.

I cooked, cleaned, and took care of siblings, bottling up my own emotions and frustrations to make things easier for the younger kids. I *had* to. I often forgot that I was the middle child—a mere child raising children—because my older sister Mia couldn't help and my eldest brother Andre didn't want to. I think my mother forgot it, too. I was a trooper, she sometimes said, and that was true: I was a good little soldier, and I was good until I could be good no longer; I was a loyal team player until my captain pushed me to the limits.

The summer when I was twelve years old, I retaliated with full-blown mutiny. I'd stopped being nice to my siblings because, deep down, I was beginning to resent them. Their existence meant that I had more responsibilities and fewer resources. We couldn't go to places or do things like other kids did, my parents would try to explain to me throughout my childhood, because there were too many of us. As a result, each announcement of a new pregnancy made my heart drop. Each kid meant more diapers, more chores, more hours of thankless work—when all I wanted was to run outdoors into the sun-drenched neighborhood and find my friends and enjoy the summer and escape from my life for a while. Instead, I got stuck at home for days on end feeling like a modern-day Cinderella.

I sat in the house one beautiful summer day, feeling the warm breeze trickle through the open window and tease my hair. My friends were somewhere out there, playing and having fun without me. It was hot out, but inside it was hotter—*I* was hotter, because I was boiling inside! *I'm not a daycare worker,* I fumed to myself, glaring around at my oblivious little siblings as they played with their toys. There was a kiddy show on TV, someone was crying over spilled juice, someone else was screaming because another someone had stolen her doll, and I felt like hurling my book out of the window. I couldn't read! I couldn't think! What sort of chaotic circus had my life become at twelve years old? *I never signed up for this. I WILL NOT stand another moment of caring for these kids. It's not my job! THEY AIN'T MY KIDS!*

My mother stepped through the door later that Saturday evening, exhausted and relieved to be home at last after her second job of cleaning houses. Her fatigue was obvious in the way she slowly stepped out of her shoes and laid her purse on the floor with a sigh. She didn't notice my angry frown.

"Hi," she called out wearily.

"Mommy!" My little sisters were overjoyed to see her. They leaped up from their toys and their snacks and rushed to give her a hug and a kiss. Her face brightened a bit, but the bags under her eyes were puffy and dark. I didn't care that she looked tired. Who had decided that she had to have all these kids and then work to support them? It had been her idea, hadn't it? The longtime frustration that had been simmering inside me boiled over like an unattended pot brimming with scalding soup.

Attempting to get attention, demanding that I be taken seriously, I scrunched up my face, deepened my voice, and walked over to glare at her, eye to eye. "I'm done!" I insisted.

My mother's face morphed into blank bewilderment. "What?"

"I'm done. I quit! I am done watching your kids."

Her lips parted and she gaped at me. Clearly this hadn't been how she'd anticipated her evening panning out.

"These are not *my kids*." I took advantage of her silence, releasing all my pent-up anger in a torrent of clipped words and steely eyes. "*I* didn't have these kids—*you* did. *You* made this choice, not me! I am not their parent—*you* are! I am not watching them anymore. I am a kid and I want to do kid things—I want to go outside, play with my friends. I am not their mother."

My mother took a deep breath. Her eyes darkened with comprehension and sadness and, finally, with empathy. She took another deep breath and let it out. "Okay," she said. "I will find another way. You don't have to do it anymore."

I didn't mince words. I flounced past her and strode toward the door, announcing that I was going outside to play.

My mom let me go. Her dependable little soldier had revolted and had caught her off guard. I blindly followed where she led most of the time, but I too had a mind of my own. I was not a master of tact or diplomacy; I was a straightforward sharpshooter and I spoke my honest mind. I suppose my mother didn't want me to lose my patience and start mistreating or spanking the kids. She chose her battles. As much as it pained her to have her child talk to her that way, she understood and gave me some breathing space.

Like Derrick, I hated my father's interpretation of parenthood. I didn't want to be a cloud. On the other hand, I hated my mother's reaction. I refused to be a tree.

If it had been just us for the rest of my childhood—my mother, my eight siblings, and myself—I think life would have been much different. We might have found a way to each discern and dislodge that broken compass inside of us sooner. Some of us may have followed a different path later in life, learning from our parents' mistakes. Maybe more of us we would have shed bad habits. Maybe we would have grown up to cultivate different attitudes, professions, and relationships. Or maybe the journey had to happen exactly as it did, meant to make us stronger and wiser than who we may have been otherwise. You can't become a butterfly without surviving as a caterpillar. You won't see the dawn if there hasn't been darkness. There can't be resurrection without death.

So maybe there's a reason for Cricket being in this story, too.

TROUBLE MAGNET

Have you ever met a trouble magnet? I bet you have. Honestly, I think I've met more than my fair share.

During my pre-teen and early teen years, Sylvester Grays had been keeping busy. My father had been in and out of prison for a while—for a year due to disorderly conduct and then soon again for another two years due to domestic abuse—and then, released once more, he returned. When I was thirteen years old, my father's thirty-something-year-old younger brother showed up at our doorstep. We knew him best by his nickname, *Cricket*. My father decided to take Cricket under his wing so "little bro" could get back on his feet.

I suppose my parents felt sorry—perhaps even partially responsible—for him. He'd grown up in the streets much like my father, a foster kid without a permanent roof over his head or a dream in his heart. He got sucked into Chicago's underworld of drug-dealing and soon after went to prison for pimping women. He had a reputation for being violent and abusive.

Now here he was, fresh out of prison and living with us.

Very quickly, Cricket lost that "little bro" status in my eyes. I could see his resemblance to our dad. It was like God molded a shorter, tougher, meaner version of Sylvester Grays, and He ran out of charismatic smiles and warm eyes by the time He got to Cricket. Cricket's gaze was cold and calculating. His smile, on the rare occasion when he flashed it, was more of a leer that always felt fake and sinister to me. A web of tattoos patterned his skin as if the ink sought to share stories he couldn't or wouldn't speak of. He reeked of cheap aftershave and smoke; though our mom wouldn't allow him to smoke in the apartment, he always did when she wasn't around. He had the hard-jawed, hard-eyed look of someone used to getting in trouble. His face and demeanor reminded me of a pit-bull.

I liked nothing about him.

Instead of sobering up and finding a job, Cricket persuaded my father to join him in a toxic cycle of drinking, partying, and loitering. The last fight my parents had before the police arrived encompassed a lot of screaming. My mom was sobbing as my father hit her. Andre wasn't home that evening. Derrick grabbed our younger brothers and I grabbed our sisters and we locked ourselves in a bedroom, trying to protect them, terrified that our dad would turn his violent wrath upon us. I remember how Derrick and I tore the sheets from the bed and made pallets on the floor, nestling between our siblings and consoling them until they fell asleep. Eventually, our mother made it to the phone somehow and called the police; Cricket watched the abuse and did nothing to stop it.

It made sense to me. Though Cricket didn't get along with me or any of my siblings, he wanted his brother's wife for himself. At thirteen years old, I was old enough to sense it in a way that made my stomach clench. He'd stare at my mom like a starving man drooling at a steak. After my dad was taken away by the police, Cricket became especially touchy with her. He'd tell her and us that she was a good woman. "How could he leave you and the kids, this beautiful family?" he'd say, lounging on the couch and glancing up from the old TV. "I won't do it. I'll stay." He'd leer at us with his ugly, yellowed teeth and help our mom carry in groceries that he couldn't wait to consume.

My uncle believed that kids were supposed to be seen and not heard. This wasn't how I'd been raised. Despite our dad's abusive tendencies toward our mom, we'd always been able to voice our opinions in the house. Cricket hated that. "Why do you let them talk to you like that?" he'd scold her. "They're kids—they need a good beating and then they won't have nothing to say." He bossed us around like he was our dad, threatening to slap us in the face if we didn't listen. Instead, we reminded him that he wasn't our dad. That only angered him further.

More than once, I came home to find him and my mother on the steps of our apartment, smoking. I was livid. In what other ways had or would he change her? And why the hell would she allow him in our home? He was a stranger; I couldn't have cared less that we shared the same blood. I didn't trust him. The longer my mother let him stay, the less I trusted her, too.

I came home from school one day and found Cricket smoking outside. I walked by him without saying hello. He reached out and grabbed my shoulder, stopping me in my tracks. A jolt of fear and disgust crackled through me.

"You're just going to disrespect me and walk along without saying anything?" he demanded.

I looked him in the eye, shook his hand off, and continued to walk up the steps toward the front door. He'd been living with my family for an entire month and he'd already managed to further screw up our already-messed-up lives. Even at that age, I had no patience for opportunists and bullies.

Cricket followed me, his face contorted with fury. "Oh, you think you're all big and bad? That you don't have to talk to me? You think I can't hurt you?"

Anger pulsed through me, giving me the strength to challenge him in turn. "What are you going to do? You're not my dad and you can't tell me what to do!"

The door to our apartment opened and my mother appeared at the top of the steps, alarmed by our raised voices.

"What's going on?"

"He's threatening me!" I cried out. "He says I have to do whatever he says around here or he'll hurt me—"

"Evonne, your brat doesn't know what the hell she's—"

"I hate him!" I interrupted his interruption. "Mom, why is he even here? He's just using us! You know that he doesn't work, he smokes all day, and he drinks like Dad! Do you think it's safe to have him living here? *I'm* not living here anymore if he is!"

I wasn't bluffing. My mom and uncle started to argue; while they were preoccupied, I stormed to the room that I shared with my mom and sisters and started to pack whatever possessions I could fit into my backpack. When I ran past my mother and Cricket on the way out, she tried to grab me and yelled at me to stay in the house. I ignored her. I knew she'd assume I'd go to a friend's house or to one of my aunts.

I went to Aunt Ledesi, who held me tightly as I wept in her arms and told her what had happened. I don't know what she told my mother, but I got to stay with her for as long as Cricket stuck around.

My uncle stayed with my family for another month. I hated that my mother chose him over me, letting me go instead of forcing him to leave. I rarely spoke to her during that month, although she bought food and brought it over to Aunt Ledesi's so that they wouldn't spend extra money to feed me. Once my mother realized that Cricket never intended to land a job, she finally tried kicking him out. They argued and he hit her. When he still refused to leave, she called the police on him. They removed Cricket from our home and he never visited again.

I didn't miss him.

...

Our uncle's departure didn't mark the end of our visiting hours. More trouble brewed on the horizon. The biggest thundercloud of our lives rolled back into town, ready to strike a familiar tree with more lightning bolts: our dad had been released from jail and, as usual, he revisited square one and tried to reconcile with our mother.

When she initially refused, he hunted down a job as a security guard at St. Stephen's Church. It was there where a sixty-year-old woman named Sister Grace developed a crush on charismatic Sylvester Grays. In the name of love (or infatuation, if you're a realist), she helped my father acquire an apartment, furniture, and a car, and even encouraged him to pursue a particular long-time dream of his.

For the next few months, my father attempted to visit my family during the weekends, trying to weasel his way back into our lives and hearts with lunch dates and little gifts. Having somewhat established himself, he again returned to my mother and persuaded her to "let him help" by taking the boys to live with him for a while. "I need another chance with *my kids*," he demanded of her when she hesitated. My mother's hands were full. She finally agreed to his proposal as long as the boys desired it. That was how all my younger brothers agreed to go live with him. My sisters visited him during the weekends.

I returned home when Cricket left; now I was devastated to find the literal creator of my daddy issues was trying to come back, too. Derrick and I steered clear of him. We knew better. I suppose we'd seen enough, we'd heard enough, we'd been hurt enough—or we'd just *had enough*; it seemed we could never get used to the cycle of abuse and forgiveness. During the weekends, I preferred spending time with Amara or my friends Aaliyah and Riley. My cousins Nala and Sanaa, ten years older than me, let me tag along with them to BBQs that they attended with their friends, and to their field hockey and track games. God knows why; I'm just grateful they did. I missed them fiercely when they went off to college and was excited to have them back when they dropped out.

I was all about escapism, whether that meant escaping to Grandma's or to Uncle Kahari's house, plugging up my ears with headphones, or diving into the pages of a good book. My favorites included the *Baby-Sitters Club* series (I felt like a lifelong babysitter myself, babysitting my siblings and sometimes—for pay—the neighbors' kids too) and *Jane Eyre* (probably my favorite novel of all time). Escapism, however, did not offer a permanent solution. *Leaving* always led to *coming back.* That was the worst part.

One of my best friends at the time—a very sweet girl named Sienna, who was my age—lived in an old house near our complex. Her older brother was Derrick's age. Her mother was Buddhist and got us both hooked on romance novels and soap operas. Romance novels by Julie Garwood, Johanna Lindsey, and Nora Roberts became my guilty pleasure, transporting me to sweet and spicy utopias. I would wrap the books in brown paper to conceal the covers so nobody would guess that my reading material included adult sex scenes (an exposed cover would lead to a *super* awkward conversation). The soap operas were bad enough as it was; my mom flipped out when she realized that I enjoyed them. "Don't watch these shows," she'd lecture me. "If you watch soap operas, your life will become a soap opera."

It's a neat theory and all, but I don't really think that's how it works. All I said was: "Really?" I was pretty sure our lives were drowning in soap opera bubbles already. I could practically feel myself suffocating.

Though it stems from the inside, I think unhappiness is tangible. It's the metallic flatness in your mouth when you can no longer enjoy the taste of food. It's the roadmap of tears on your face when you cry yourself to sleep each night. It's the sound of music blasting in your ears when you're trying to drown out emotions you no longer want to feel. It's the pause where your laughter should be inserted but isn't. It's the sight of someone who shows up time and time again to kick you in the stomach right when you've picked yourself up and glued yourself back together.

It's a fourteen-year-old face in the mirror that stares back at you with death in her eyes.

12

BREATHING SPACE

I'd never have thought Andre would be the one to save me, but life is funny like that. If it wasn't for Andre, the bully of our family, I would have never fulfilled that hazy dream of someday going to college. If it wasn't for Andre, in a sense, I wouldn't be around to write this book either.

But back then, there in the small bathroom with its chipped porcelain and ragged bath rug, I believed myself hopeless. I braced against the sink, the little white bottle clutched in one hand. *Why? Why is this my life? Why was I born into this? Why are we poor? Why is Mom always taking him back?* The girl in the mirror stared back at me. She had no answers to offer. She wept along with me. *I don't want to live like this! What's the point? Nobody listens to me! Nobody loves me! I hate myself. I hate my family. I hate it all!*

It is remarkable how lonely you can feel even when constantly surrounded by people. It is eerie how life is dictated by luck—the luck of which family you are born into. I had friends who had stable households, loving parents, families who always made time for them, normal siblings, and access to ballet lessons, summer camp, and nice clothes. I, on the other hand, lived in the heart of chaos. I felt neglected, unseen, and forced to grow up fast. I'd tried running away a few times. I'd tried staying with my relatives for as long as I was able. I always ended up back home.

Would they even notice if I was gone? Would they even care?

I'd be one less kid to worry about. One less mouth to feed. There were so many of us anyway. And I would be free...free from the pain, neglect, emptiness...free from my returning father.

Derrick would care. I felt a pang of regret that I would leave my best friend behind. I thought about my younger sisters. Would they hate me for abandoning them as our dad had abandoned us? Would they be able to take care of themselves without me? Maybe my parents would have regrets. Maybe my mom would feel horrible for ignoring me. Maybe she would cry over my little dead body and wish she'd treated me nicer. She would tell my dad and he would feel like it was his fault. He'd have to live with the regret for his entire life.

Yes. Good. It would serve them right.

I wondered if I would go to Hell. According to the Bible, God would damn me for taking my own life. It was a sin. The fires would be hot...there would be pitch forks, torture, and demons...

My hands started to shake. I couldn't get myself to open the bottle of pills.

Or maybe God would take pity on me. Maybe he'd take me up to Heaven so I could finally be happy. That would be a very different sort of afterlife. I envisioned blue skies and sunny fields of lush green grass, colorful flowers and refreshing rivers, beautiful smiling angels and music. I would be able to fly in Heaven, it would be a place filled with enchanting music, and I would be given everything I'd ever wanted in my life. I wouldn't be poor. I wouldn't cry myself to sleep at night. I wouldn't need to live with my father ever again.

I can't take it anymore. I can't, I can't, I can't...

A knock on the door startled me. "Connie?" Andre's voice drifted through the keyhole. "What are you doing in there?"

I paused. He had seen me go in. I'd pushed past him while I'd been crying. Had he seen the pill bottle? "None of your business!"

"Open the door!" he said.

"No!" I retorted.

"Open the door! Open it *now*!"

His demands and his frantic knocking incited a fresh wave of tears. The enormity of what I was about to do frightened me. His frantic awareness of it frightened me even further.

"No," I kept saying. My hands were shaking so badly that it was difficult to get the cap off the bottle, but I finally managed. "No!" This was what I wanted, right? *Yes,* I told myself. This was what I needed. There couldn't be any turning back. *They won't change,* I reprimanded myself. *Nothing will change. Only I can change this.* It wasn't a bad thing. I hadn't contemplated death too much, but I hoped that it would be like swimming out of blackness and into the light, like a butterfly emerging from a cocoon. Surely it would be better than all this.

I've wondered, since then, why so many people choose bathrooms as a suicide setting. There are many reasons to choose from, probably. Bathrooms are where pills and razors are located. They are private spaces, where other people are far less likely to interrupt you or bang down the door if they think you're taking your sweet time flossing or grappling with constipation. Bathrooms are also easier to clean, since water is in great supply. Then there's the mirror, too, offering a final face-down and farewell.

For my fourteen-year-old self, this bathroom had become a narrow ledge at the world's end. I teetered on the cliff between hope and despair, reeling from my never-ending exposure to a world of violence and vulnerability where no one seemed to care and no one seemed to notice.

From my vantage point, there was only one way out: step off the cliff and into the void. I wasn't sure yet if falling meant flying.

"I saw you with those pills!" Andre bellowed. "Open the door!"

"Connie!" my mother shouted through the door. Andre had gotten her attention and she had realized that something terrible was happening. "Let us in! Let us in right now, Connie!"

I knew the pills would kill me. Seven years ago, when I was just seven years old, I'd seen my sister Mia—nineteen years old at the time—overdose on a bottle of pills. She had to get her stomach pumped. She would have died if they hadn't gotten her to the hospital in time. It had been her second attempt at suicide; she, too, had attempted to kill herself as a fourteen-year-old. My father's drunken fights and our mother's anger had pushed Mia to the brink, triggering her depression as her mental illness began to surface as well.

I spilled the pills into my palm just as Andre kicked down the door with his foot. It fell to the side, propelled by the force of his kick, before it fell toward me. Andre and my mother rushed at me before I could react. My mother swatted my hand away, hurling the bottle to the floor. The pills spilled everywhere, patterning the floor like plastic white flower petals.

I sobbed as they scattered. Why couldn't everybody leave me alone? Why didn't they ignore me now, the only time I wanted them to? Why couldn't they just let me go?

"Baby, what are you trying to do?" My mother ignored the ruined door and the scattered pills. She grabbed me into her embrace and held me close. "Baby, why?"

"I don't want this." I realized that I was shaking. I might have fallen if she hadn't been holding me up. I could barely see through the tears. "I don't want him to come back."

"Is that what this is all about?" she demanded, at last addressing the issue of my depression. "Is this about your father? I know you don't want this to happen. You don't want him to come back." She caressed my hair soothingly. "But everything's going to be okay."

It wouldn't be okay. Life had been far from perfect without my dad, but we'd sort of found our footing. I felt I could deal with my depression if he wasn't around. We all knew how he continuously cheated on my mother, how he cheated on our entire family, how he kicked us aside whenever he wanted to live it up in L.A. with friends and girlfriends. Somehow, our mom didn't care. She opened the door to him every time, welcoming all the hurt, resentment, and chaos that he brought in.

"Why are you taking him back?"

"I'm sorry, Connie—it's hard for you, but you know that it's best for our family. It's going to be okay."

I started to cry again. "Be *okay*?"

"Yes," she said. "I need help. This is his way of helping us; he's going to be there for us. That's why he took on your brothers, and that's also why he's coming back to us. We will be a family again. You're growing up, Connie. You need to be a big girl. You've got to find a way to forgive your dad."

Big girl? The phrase pierced my ears like a curse. I'd been a "big girl" for as long as I could remember.

It took years for me to fully digest that my mother had, too. She'd worked hard—really hard. Before she was surrounded by a pack of children and a mountain of chores, she'd had a good job in the local school system. She'd cared for her nephews and nieces while Aunt Ledesi went to night school to become a teacher, and would buy clothes for Nala and Sanaa with her meager earnings. My parents didn't believe in birth control, obviously, believing it blasphemous. Each fight with my father broke my mother's heart, and it came to feel like each pregnancy was a plea for him to stay, to grow more attached to the family, to commit. Each time, this plea went unheard. Each time, the rubber band snapped away further. He left and my mother stayed: determined yet despairing, a broken child raising lonely children.

She did what she had to do. And, learning from her example, so did the rest of us. We survived. But surviving was not enough for me. I wanted to thrive.

My mother made me promise I'd never try to commit suicide again—that I'd tell her if I ever had such thoughts so she could help me. Andre and I never spoke of it, but I sensed in him a newfound awareness and something akin to compassion. He stopped stealing my cassette tapes to record over them with his music. He no longer went out of his way to say hurtful things to me. In his own way, he seemed to empathize with my pain.

Andre and my mother foiled my attempt to die. They gave me a second chance at life. In a way—literally—they gave me this breathing space.

13

TRANSITIONS

There is a story about a child who stumbles across a butterfly cocoon while walking through the woods; delighted with her discovery, she brings it home with her to watch the beautiful transformation that she has been told will soon take place. She leaves the cocoon on the kitchen counter and waits. A few days go by without any sign of life from the cocoon. Then, one day, the cocoon begins to writhe frantically. Impatient or concerned about the butterfly's strength, the little girl decides to help. She slits open a bit of the cocoon and the butterfly slips out, motionless and wilted.

Growing up, I had a fondness for butterflies as well, but I knew better than to try to cage or control wild things. I played in the gardens of Balboa Park with my cousins and friends, and I had time to study the animal kingdom when I secured a summer job as a teenager at the San Diego zoo. The laws of nature made sense to me. Ironically enough, nobody seemed to have any qualms about trying to cage or control me and my siblings.

My parents' decisions, misinformed or impulsive as they were, had great consequences on my entire family. They certainly played their share in the formation of our individual characters, values, and belief systems. We turned out the way we did partially because of our parents, just as their own individual pasts helped to carve out their paths as well.

...

A week or so after my suicide attempt, our father showed up. He attempted to make amends with me by taking me out to lunch and shopping at the mall. "Your dad's trying to reach out," my mother pointed out when I refused to get dressed that morning. "You should go. Give him another chance."

Another chance. How sick I was of that phrase. This would be their third "chance" after two official divorces. *No,* I wanted to yell at my mom. *Why another chance? We were finally doing okay without him! We were getting used to this life and then he comes along to shake up every little thing.* But I got dressed and got ready. I went out to lunch and to the mall with him. He apologized, talking about how he wanted to make things right again and how this time would be different. He attempted to make small talk and to bribe me with presents; I tried to survive the afternoon.

What could I do? Betrayal was a sucker punch to the gut, but all my life I'd been told that blood ran thicker than water. He was my dad.

At the food court of the mall, I sat across the table from a man I no longer really knew or even liked.

"I'm sorry, Constance." He attempted to apologize somewhere between ordering our burgers and asking for extra ketchup. "You got my letters, didn't you? Can you forgive me for not being around?"

"The letters you sent me from jail? Yeah, I got those."

"Oh. Well, you never wrote back. I wasn't sure."

Of course I'd never written back. I'd stopped reading them after the very first letter and threw each one away when it arrived without a second glance. I didn't want to feel anything for him. I knew him for what he was: a liar, a deceiver, a fake. I couldn't trust a word he said. He wanted me to be like my mother, to just accept him back into my heart with open arms and without questions.

I couldn't.

I stared at him and didn't reply. I wanted a *dad*: a real, compassionate, accountable, present, sober, loving parent and role model. A stranger stared back at me instead, desperate to be accepted and liked, hiding his true self and motives beneath a veneer of friendly chatter.

"How's school?"

"Fine."

"Do you like your teachers?"

"Sure."

"How about your friends? What are they like? What do you enjoy doing with them on the weekends?"

"Stuff."

He had no idea that I was excelling in my classes because I didn't want to end up like him. He had no idea that I had made a pledge in my diary that I'd never let a man beat me or talk smack to me as he did to my mother. He had no idea that my favorite novel was *Jane Eyre* or that my favorite family moments no longer involved him. I later learned that he promised he'd "make it up to me" when my mom informed him of my suicide attempt, but he was too much of a coward to bring it up in front of me. He knew nothing, because how can you know anything when you're not around to make memories and learn things about the people you're supposed to love?

Maybe our outing made him feel better. Maybe it assuaged his guilt and helped him feel worthy of coming back to us. My guard never lowered. My heart never peeked out from its cocoon. That was another thing I'd learned from him. You can't force anyone to love you. You can't force anyone to stay. I no longer wanted him. He'd never wanted us. So why the hell was he back? I knew my father for what he was: a harbinger of change and heartbreak and abuse, however good his intentions.

I was helpless to stop him.

A month later, my parents had officially remarried for the third time, secretly legitimizing their reunion at the local courthouse and telling no one until the deed had been done. My father uprooted us midsummer and moved us to a house in Firethorn, a town in San Diego that was thirty minutes away. Life as we knew it changed—exactly as I'd feared it would. I felt torn away from Riley and Aaliyah and the rest of my friends; my beloved school, my favorite teacher, and familiar surroundings all faded away. Instead I got a new neighborhood, a new school, unfamiliar faces, and a "new beginning" that felt as dry and tasteless as old taffy.

The house in Firethorn was huge in comparison to the apartments we had lived in before. It was two stories, and included five bedrooms and three bathrooms. Realizing my state of mind, my mother wisely decided that I deserved—for the first time in my life—a room all to myself. My siblings weren't at all happy with the idea that I got to have my own room—a cramped attic space with a sloped ceiling—while they continued to share. I treasured my hard-won privacy and morphed the space into my sanctuary, knowing that I deserved it.

A couple of weeks before school began, we had finally settled in. The weather had been beautifully summery and warm. Our neighborhood was prettier, and there was a small park across the street where my brothers liked to hang out and play basketball. I sometimes liked to walk barefoot in the grass and watch the bees and butterflies dance above the park's wildflowers and the neighbors' rose gardens. It was lonely, though, so I didn't do it often, preferring to read in my room instead. Apart from my siblings, I didn't really know anyone in the neighborhood.

I was home one day when someone knocked gently on our front door. I went and opened it, wondering if one of my brothers had locked himself out or if the police were here because my father had done something to enrage the neighborhood. Instead, a girl stared back at me. She looked to be about my age, though she was actually a year older.

"Hi." She beamed at me cheerfully. She had a broad smile and beautiful, kind eyes. "My name's Samantha."

"Hi," I replied. "I'm Connie."

"Would you like to be friends?"

My heart smiled, and the smile reached my face. "Okay."

Hers was a simple statement, and one I accepted just as simply. Children's laws of life may be cruel, but they are rarely complex. There's a beautiful honesty and simplicity in "childish" transactions that often fades as we get older and colder.

"I live across the street with my parents and little brother," she added. "You should come visit."

She won me over with her genuine smile and warm eyes. I had moved into this neighborhood with a sour predisposition and a bad premonition. Samantha's kindness cleared up the storms in my heart a little. I told her about my family and how we'd ended up moving to Firethorn. I explained how my parents had gotten back together and that we'd moved to be a "family" again.

"I hate it," I confessed. "I had to leave all my friends behind. Now I have to start off at a new school all by myself."

"Well, don't worry about that." Samantha squeezed my hand. "You have me now, so you won't be starting off at a new school all by yourself. I'll show you around."

Samantha was true to her word. I met her family and fell in love with her compassionate parents. Even her little brother, quintessentially annoying (even if only due to the fact that he was the little brother and being annoying came with the job), seemed like a good kid. A few days later, we walked to school together. I stood up straight and held my head high, feeling I wasn't alone. Samantha turned out to be my first and truest friend in high school, and we bonded over teenage crushes, movies, music, and books. She introduced me to her friends and encouraged me to join the varsity cheerleading team.

I survived the move. I survived the year. I didn't attempt to commit suicide again in my life. Despite the relief that it might have brought from worldly suffering, I realized that, at the end of the day, suicide was the wrong move. It was an act of abandonment, of leaving your loved ones behind prematurely. How did that make me better than my father?

Even more than that, it *was* a sin. Not in the conventional way, maybe; I no longer believed that committing suicide automatically put you on the train to Hell. But ending your life meant throwing away the most precious thing God could ever give you: potential. I didn't choose the life I was born into, but I became determined that I would find a way to change it or die trying. Even in my darkest moments, suicide no longer felt like a real option.

I realized, somehow, that it wasn't the right sort of "out" for me.

...

In the story of the child and the butterfly, the butterfly was lucky. But it wasn't just luck.

The little girl had realized her mistake in nearly killing the insect. Alarmed and unsure, she'd decided that the best thing would be to gently place the butterfly back in the cocoon and let it emerge by itself whenever it was ready. Her mother helped her place a drop of honey on the slit she'd made to seal the cocoon shut. The next day, the child noticed that the cocoon was moving. She did not touch it. The butterfly struggled and struggled; at last it broke free, emerging and stretching its spectacular wings. It wobbled around a bit and then fluttered up, flying away as the little girl watched, amazed and delighted.

Such was my brush with death. Death had been prodding my cocoon, offering to give me a way out before realizing that it was not the right way. I realized it, too. There could be better exits and escapes than taking one's own life, and I promised myself that I would find them. Someday my *real* life would begin; I had to be patient and strong. I thought of my soul as a secret garden, hidden from sight and from the cruel weather elements. When the sun emerged and spring appeared, my garden would come to life, and pink and white roses and camellias would unfurl their petals and soak the world in their fragrance. Then my heart would drink from them, fluttering free and carefree, never again needing to hide in a shadowy cocoon.

Looking back now, I am very grateful I hadn't "freed" myself prematurely, for that would not have represented the true freedom that I sought and deserved. I sensed at the time—though it would take me years to be able to write it down in words—that the whole point of life is to overcome, to struggle, to *break through and beyond,* to fly free into the limitless universe where all things are possible. You have to fight and accept your scars if you are to shed your skin and emerge as something stronger, fiercer, more beautiful, with wings.

Survive the darkness of the cocoon, and you will emerge into the light of day.

14

A LIFE UPENDED

Despite my father being back, I was determined to live my life to the fullest. I jumped at any opportunity to escape the house. Just like old times, Sanaa took me with her on a weekend outing to a beach BBQ. This time, though, Nala didn't come. We went with Sanaa's friend Gabrielle, and my little brother Michael tagged along, too. We decided to head back around 4 p.m. to escape the worst of the traffic. Gabrielle eased her cute compact car out of the parking spot and headed toward the main road. She paused at a stop sign, looked both ways, and eased along forward. Traffic let up and she began to drive a bit faster. We entered a ramp that led to the freeway. The car in front of us suddenly slowed, forcing Gabrielle to do the same.

Sanaa rummaged in her bag and pulled out a tube of lip gloss. She coated her lips and asked, "You guys want to do this again next weekend?"

We didn't get a chance to answer.

The next thing I knew, my body lurched forward as if the entire world had suddenly stopped twirling on its axis and I hadn't—and I collided against the world. The seatbelt bit into my waist, but it could restrain only the lower portion of my body. My ears filled with the sickening crunch of metal on metal and my face smashed grotesquely into the driver's seat in front of me, then bounced off and smashed into the window, blackening my vision for a long moment.

...

The day your life gets upended doesn't come with spoiler alerts.

You don't roll out of bed in the morning with a neon sign taped to your window, the words *Don't get up—go back to bed!* blazing at you in warning. You don't realize that this might be the last day in a long time when you'll be eating your breakfast cereal in such a carefree way, confident in the knowledge that though there are things beyond your control (e.g., your father's violence, your mother's tantrums, your family's relocation around town), there *are* things you *do* fully control: your choice of reading material, how quickly or how slowly you eat your cereal, the direction of your footsteps and the timing of when you sit down. You go about your business like a normal fifteen-year-old without considering the repercussions of a sleepless night or an emotional breakdown. You might even get in a car and head out for a daytrip to Mission Beach for some late summer fun.

You go willingly, happily. You never suspect you'll come back changed.

At least that's how it happened with me. Mission Beach, just a thirty-minute drive from home, is lovely in the summer. It also gets jam-packed in August. My cousin Sanaa and her best friend Gabrielle showed up that morning around 10 a.m. to pick me up. We planned to head out early to find a parking spot, wanting to beat the oppressive heat and the traffic. Gabrielle paused her tiny compact car by the curb and tooted gently on the horn. Sanaa got out and jogged up to the house, poking her head in at the door. "Connie? You ready to go?"

"Yes!" I finished adjusting my shorts and tank top over my bikini, then rushed to the door.

"Okay…you have everything?"

"Yes."

"Oh—y'all going to the beach!" Michael chased after me, cradling a basketball under one arm. "Sanaa, can I come? I wanna play ball!"

Really? I rolled my eyes and shot Sanaa what I hoped would be a telepathic message: *Please say no.*

Sweet as ever, Sanaa smiled and nodded. She didn't get my message. "It's fine with me," she said. "Aunt Kay, that okay with you?"

Mom looked up from where she was sorting through some bills on the table. She offered us a tired smile. "Michael can go."

I tried to hide my disappointment as Michael skipped out the door. Sanaa and I followed after him. "We'll be home around five or so," Sanaa added with a wave at my mom.

Michael and I strapped ourselves into the back seat of the car, grinning like Cheshire cats on the way to Wonderland. I was too excited to be annoyed at Michael for long. Sanaa, like Nala, was in her mid-twenties at the time. Both sisters had dropped out of college. Sanaa worked in retail and never went back to school; Nala, who had gotten pregnant during freshman year, later made a comeback and earned her master's. I was overjoyed when the two of them moved back in with my aunt because it meant that I would see more of them myself. They were beautiful, outgoing, and knew all about sports and guys; having grown up in the same apartment complex, I had always looked up to them. Though ten years older than me—and ten times nicer than most twenty-something-year-olds—they always made me feel welcome and included in their excursions. I knew that this beautiful day at a beach BBQ with Sanaa and Gabrielle would be no exception.

The first portion of that day is locked in my mind like a beloved old photograph tucked away within a book for safekeeping. A light breeze blew at our hair and kissed our skin, keeping the sun's heat at bay. The

BBQ infused the beach with the zesty aromas of sizzling sausage and hamburgers. Boisterous laughter and animated chatter surrounded us. Michael and I drank soda while Sanaa and Gabrielle sipped from wine coolers. We snacked until our fingers were greasy and our bellies were full, then washed our hands and faces in the sea.

Michael ran off to join other hopeful pro-basketball players, finally leaving us girls in peace. I settled down with Sanaa and Gabrielle on towels that we stretched over the ground, our colorful patchwork of cloths like a magical carpet on an undulating tan sky of sand. Sanaa and Gabrielle shared stories about funny characters they'd met at work and about the cute boys in their lives, causing me to giggle.

"How 'bout you, Connie?" Gabrielle teased. "You been winking at anybody special lately?"

"There was this guy," I told them, wanting to share something. "But he didn't turn out to be that great."

"What happened?" they asked.

Thanks to Samantha, I had acclimated to my new high school pretty fast. She'd encouraged me to join the varsity cheerleading team with her; I did, cheering our school's footballers on like I used to cheer on Derrick in the little leagues we attended when we were younger (Derrick unfortunately didn't attend my school; he finished his senior year at the old school, where my mom dropped him off on her way to work). And while on the cheerleading team, during the first season at my new school, I had developed a crush on one of the school's football players.

It turned out that he liked me, too. *Hi,* he'd addressed me outside the locker rooms one day. *My name's Jason. And you are...?*

Constance.

You look real cute in that outfit. Haven't seen you around here before. You just moved in the area? I'd never thought my purple-and-yellow cheerleading uniform was anything to crow about, but suddenly I felt it suited me perfectly. Samantha had been right about urging me to join the cheerleading team—it *was* fun. *Wanna hang out sometime? Can I have your number?*

He looked good and seemed nice; I gave him my number. I cheered for his varsity team, so we saw each other on the field frequently. He called me a couple times to chat. I enjoyed the butterflies that fluttered in my stomach whenever he spoke to me. Sadly, those super-excited butterflies crumbled to dust when he tried to pressure me into having sex on our first date.

Nuh-uh, I'd thought to myself. *Too strong. Too fast.*

Hell no.

I was only fifteen years old, but I was old enough to know my own mind. I'd hit puberty three years ago; my mom had soothed my terror at seeing blood in my underwear by treating me to a "womanhood celebration" that consisted of ice cream and an outing with her and Aunt Ledesi, followed by The Talk: *Sex is wrong outside of marriage; God will send you to Hell if you have premarital sex; once you have sex with someone you are tied to their spirit, yadda yadda…*I didn't really need The Talk. The morality of adolescent abstinence aside, I'd grown up around more than enough newborns to understand the possible repercussions of sex; judging from my parents' rollercoaster of pregnancies and crying kids, it wasn't worth it. I also had a hunch that God was keeping a close eye on me anyway and that He didn't really like me much to begin with (if He did, why had I been born into this family with all its problems?). I had no intention of inciting further wrath by doing something He apparently found so inappropriate.

The next day, the footballer began dating another girl—one whom I'd considered a good friend of mine. The sight saddened me and hurt my feelings, but I didn't regret my choice for a second. On the contrary, I believed that it steeled my resolve. I was never a fan of peer pressure.

"Whatever," Sanaa said once I finished my story. "His loss." She pulled out a deck of cards from her purse. "You remember how to play spades?" I grinned and nodded, grateful that she'd changed the subject.

We played. I kept losing, but I was having too much fun to care. When we tired of cards, we played dominos. Later we lay back on our towels and drank in the sun, chatting about things we wanted to do and far-off places we wanted to go see.

That was it, and that was enough.

If happiness was a tangible thing, it would have the face of my loved ones on the beach that day, and the aroma of the salty sea and of fresh-cooked hamburgers, and it would sound like joyful laughter and crashing waves.

...

When that other vehicle collided into us, I don't know how many seconds or minutes I was out of it. When I opened my eyes, the girls were shaking and panting. Next to me, Michael rubbed his head and whimpered. My own head was throbbing. I touched my face and skull, expecting blood or bits of brain to appear on my fingers; my hands came away clean.

"What happened?" I rasped. "My head hurts…"

We tumbled out of the car, the driver behind us doing the same. He hadn't been paying attention when we slowed. As a result, his car had collided violently into the rear of Gabrielle's, completely totaling the back. The four of us had lurched forward from the impact, Michael and I both slamming our heads against the front seats. We stood together outside the crumpled little car and waited for the police to arrive, cradling our heads and our belongings. My headache refused to go away.

Upon our return home, we'd shaken off the worst of the shock. My mother patted us down, her face pinched with worry. "Does anything hurt?" she demanded of us. "Anything at all?"

"Well, my head hurts," I told her. "I hit it against the seat and window. But that's all."

"Yeah," Michael complained. "My head hurts, too."

All things considered, we felt fine. We told our parents that nobody had really gotten hurt. We hadn't even broken a bone. I thought my stint as a five-year-old Wonder Woman had been more eventful than this.

Our parents took us to the hospital the next morning, just in case. Someone had mentioned that we might not get insured for the crash if we didn't get checked. Still, the doctors didn't find something wrong with me at the time. I had a stupendous headache, but what else would be expected after a violent car crash? We'd been very lucky, everyone told me and Michael. We hadn't broken any bones or fractured any body parts. We hadn't even bled. I had suffered from a concussion, the doctors said, and I shouldn't have been allowed to sleep the night before. But I had; I luckily was okay nonetheless. That was obvious enough, wasn't it?

It had just been an accident, Michael and I consoled each other. We weren't in trouble. It wasn't our fault. No one had been drinking or pulling off any dangerous stunts. We'd been hit, but I thought I hadn't really gotten hurt.

I wish I'd been right.

15

TONIC CLONIC

Imagine being the pilot of a small plane. You're commanding the machinery, flying over incredible vistas. Sometimes this trip can be a breathtaking, perilous, and beautiful experience—especially whenever you stop to consider the awesome notion that you're flying in a chair in the freaking sky. Life can be amazing like that.

After a while, as a seasoned pilot, flying becomes routine. You get so good at it that it feels like second nature, like breathing or swallowing. You don't have to think twice about breathing, do you? Just so, as a pilot, you know what all the buttons do and when to press them; you don't need to think twice. You run the plane on autopilot.

Then one day, and for no fathomable reason, everything fades to black. You feel like you're about to drop. You *are* dropping. A dark nightmare of a storm surrounds you—where the heck did it come from?—and the scariest thing is that it literally came out of nowhere.

Lights in the plane start blinking, the warning sirens begin blaring, and the aircraft begins to shake and convulse. It flings itself right and left and upside down without your consent—*without your knowledge.* You have no part in that. You have no say. You can't do anything. You don't know what is happening in the plane because you've lost consciousness. When the plane stops and the nightmare ends and you wake up again, you find yourself in an unfamiliar land with no sense of direction. Worst of all, you remember nothing of what just took place.

And the nightmare isn't over yet.

Slowly, slowly, you begin to reorient yourself: you're lying on the floor. Slowly, you begin remembering why you're surrounded by buttons and what these buttons do: these are the cognitive functions of your brain. You realize that you completely blacked out, that you're extremely tired, and that your tongue is throbbing with pain and bleeding. Why is it bleeding?

It bleeds because you bit it.

Waking up is a disturbing experience. There's a sense of disorientation and vulnerability and pain and confusion that all collide together like toxic little atoms, forming a huge black hole of terror that threatens to swallow you whole and destroy you. It is gut-wrenchingly terrifying.

Once you've landed, your brain—the engine of the plane, so to speak—gets scanned and examined and tested. Bruises have blossomed across your body. You're in a foreign location—a hospital?—and you can't understand how you got here. Neurologists scratch their chins or throw their hands up in the air like perplexed mechanics. Often—as in my case—there's no obvious cause that could explain the temporary malfunction of the plane. It's not always easy to describe it. It's even harder learning to live and cope with it. There's no guarantee that it won't happen again. In fact, it's very likely that it will.

The diagnosis is presented eventually: *generalized epilepsy.*

Two weeks after the car accident that totaled Gabrielle's car and gave me a concussion, I lost control. The first incidence happened in the kitchen of our home, in the presence of my mom and Michael. I held a glass of water and was walking toward the sink to drop it off. Suddenly the top of my body was shaking and jerking; though I didn't know it at the time, these initial tremors were "simple partial seizures." It was as if there was an earthquake taking place *inside me*, with tectonic plates clashing within my hands and radiating out from me as frightening vibrations. The glass fell to the tile floor and shattered into dozens of pieces. I didn't exactly lose consciousness that time—it was more of a quick fading and coming-to of senses, where I held the glass one moment and found it in shatters on the floor the next.

...

Later that summer, I began working at a paid internship position at California's Employment Development Department (EDD). Samantha and her mother, Evelyn, already worked there; they'd helped me apply and get in via a Youth At Work program. It was a lovely environment with nice people, and I enjoyed the work. It felt fulfilling to know that I was part of a team who helped other people find jobs and get back on their feet. I observed how people, given the right resources, could and did seize such opportunities to level up in life and make something of themselves. I was proud of them—and of myself, for being a tiny part of this process.

I looked forward to the thirty-minute-long commute every morning and afternoon, carpooling with Samantha and her mom, Evelyn, because it meant I could share some extra time with them. Evelyn was the sort of person who always had a smile for you, and it shone out of her face like a sunray. Like Samantha, she was petite, chubby, and sassy. She always spoke her mind and meant what she said, but her abruptness was tempered by her empathy and generosity of spirit. She wore her brown hair bobbed and curly, and loved to accessorize her colorful outfits with bold earrings and gold necklaces that suited her optimistic and outgoing personality.

A couple of weeks after that first bout of strange tremors in the kitchen—the doctors hadn't been able to diagnose anything that day after my dad had taken me to the hospital—I'd shown up to work one sunny morning in my favorite summer dress and a happy disposition. The office buzzed with life. People were being productive, deadlines were being met, good things were happening. I stood up and grabbed a folder that someone had told me to deliver, then began to walk across the room to go put it on a desk.

I never made it to the desk.

Darkness overwhelmed me as my vision faded to black. The next thing I knew, I was sprawled face-up on the floor, disoriented and terrified. There were people with confused and scared expressions surrounding me, and someone was yelling something about calling an ambulance. Then, a familiar face: Evelyn had pushed through the crowd that had gathered around me and she was on her knees next to me, stroking my head and looking petrified.

"Connie, I called your mom," she said, visibly fighting to stay calm. "Your dad is on his way to take you to the hospital. Are you okay?"

My mouth was full of blood from my bleeding, throbbing tongue, and my head hurt from where I'd hit it on the floor when I'd fallen. Tears spurted from my eyes. They blurred my dizzy vision, making me feel even more vulnerable and afraid. I would later learn that this had been my first tonic-clonic seizure. The doctors would run tests on me that day, as they would for weeks and months and years later. First they gave me Valproate, which caused me to break out in a rash and did not control the seizures. Then they prescribed Lamictal, which initially caused my hands to shake and made me dizzy, lethargic, and forgetful. I did find some relief in Keppra (and use it to this day), but that has its complications too.

It would take me years to gain back control.

. . .

I'm an epileptic. Let me explain.

The medical term for my condition is "generalized epilepsy" characterized by "tonic-clonic" seizures, a term that is used more often these days than "grand mal." Maybe *grand mal* sounds too scary; it does translate to "big bad" after all. There are actually a dozen types of epilepsy; the type you have determines the sort of seizures you get. Tonic-clonic seizures are arguably the least fun. They belong in the "generalized seizures" category; they are the most noticeable of them all. A tonic-clonic seizure has two phases. In the tonic phase—which lasts a few seconds—your skeletal muscles tense, pushing or pulling your hands and feet away from your body. If you're standing or even sitting, you will inevitably fall. The storm has been unleashed; the plane begins to plummet. Sometimes air will be forcefully expelled from your lungs, so you'll emit an involuntary moan or other such noise. You'll likely lose full consciousness. You'll scare the people around you who don't have a clue what the hell is going on. You might even scare the people who do.

The next phase is the clonic one. The storm builds up, the earth-quake gets stronger, and you're at the mercy of the haywire plane. Your muscles begin to contract and relax rapidly, ensuing in convulsions. You might experience light tremors, exaggerated twitches of the body. Or maybe you'll be hit by something much more powerful: a violent vibrating and quaking of your stiffened extremities. Your body might roll around on the ground and your limbs might stretch. Your eyes will probably roll back or close. It's likely that you'll bite your tongue and hurt yourself due to violent jaw contractions. Can't feel it yet? Don't worry. The pain will engulf you once you come to your senses.

Waking up, it's likely that your brain and body will be exhaust-ed. So much so that you will probably fall into a postictal sleep. That means that you're in an altered state of consciousness, characterized by drowsiness, hypertension, nausea, confusion, disorientation, migraines, temporary amnesia, and other such delightful symptoms. This goes on for anywhere between five and thirty-five minutes, give or take. If the mental trauma overwhelms you, don't be surprised if you throw up or burst into tears.

Your loved ones will be terrified, especially if this is the first time that you've gone all zombie-touches-electric-fence on them. This does nothing to make you less petrified. Your family calls 911 or rushes you to the hospital. The doctors perform a number of incomprehensible tests on you and you must be patient—for days, for weeks, for years—as you undergo blood tests, urine tests, and brain scans with big scary titles like the electroencephalogram (EEG for short). Unlike the mechanics rummaging around in the belly of a busted plane, doctors can't just trade your hippocampus for another or use a wrench on a damaged hot spot in your brain. They can go for all the MRIs and EEGs and CAT scans they want and map your brain to the fullest, but they can't see beneath a landscape of the obvious. They can't pick apart the engine of your brain to find why it has its fits and stutters—they're scared, and rightfully so, of doing more harm than good.

Here's what they do know and what they will tell you: seizures happen when one or more parts of the brain experience a burst of abnormal electrical signals that interrupt normal signals, essentially screwing up the brain's streamlined functions. Seizures can occur thanks to an imbalance of brain chemicals, a brain tumor, brain damage from an injury or illness, or a stroke. Epilepsy is a neurological disorder marked by recurring seizures. Generalized epilepsy means that there is no obvious cause, meaning that there's no respective obvious cure or even treatment.

The doctors will attempt to help. They'll keep you in the hospital overnight. You might get a Dr. Pingle by your side, like I did: a tall, kind-faced man with a pale face and a deep, reassuring voice that unfortunately had nothing reassuring to tell me. Your doctor might point to pictures of brain scan procedures and you might burst into terrified tears. You don't want all those electrodes attached to your scalp. That's what happens in science fiction thrillers before the aliens dissect the person's brain and body, right? You don't want to be inserted into the circular white coffin that they call the MRI machine, because what if you don't come out?

Don't worry, though. You do.

You'll try the medications, too, of course, because you have to try something. These can come with horrific side effects: liver damage, hair loss, and even—oh the irony!—seizures (to name a few). For the record, birth control won't really work on you. You will still have bouts of epilepsy throughout high school until you find the right medication to regain control. You'll never really know when a fit will overtake you. One day during your junior year of high school, for example, you might find yourself in the girl's green-tiled bathroom, coming out of the stall and walking toward the porcelain sink, and you'll suddenly get really dizzy and black out. You'll wake up with the school nurse hovering over you, with a blanket under your head and another covering your body. There will be blood and pain in your mouth because you chewed your tongue, there will be urine on the floor and shame in your heart because you lost control of your bowel movements, and there will be three other girls in the bathroom staring down at you like *you're* some sort of disease.

In part, you can understand the horror, ridicule, disgust, and sympathy that you see in the faces around you, but you can't forgive it. You've never felt so alienated in your entire life. It isn't enough that the world has turned against you; your body has, too. You scare people, including yourself.

Welcome to my world.

Finding out I had epilepsy changed everything for me. My life no longer felt like it was mine. Ever since I could remember, other people had made choices on my behalf: what family I'd be born into, where I'd grow up, whose hand-me-downs I'd wear, what school I'd attend, which portion of dinner was mine, and so on.

Suddenly, I lost control over the one thing that nobody else had the right to govern: my body.

The vulnerability, fear, and sense of otherness sucked me back into a cesspool of depression. My parents didn't really talk about my condition; for them, it was just something I had and something to cope with. I turned to my friends and teachers for support and comfort because they took the time to initiate conversations that mattered. They encouraged me to keep going despite my condition. They reassured me that I could live a normal life. They pointed out that Lewis Carroll,

Charles Dickens, and Edgar Allen Poe were epileptic. So was Theodore Roosevelt, who loved to spend time outdoors despite his many health conditions. Flo-Jo was an epileptic Olympian athlete. Prince was an epileptic emperor of pop.

That's how it is. You have no choice but to push through and get used to your new reality. You still get up in the morning, go to school, go to work, deal with your family, interact with your friends, ride the bus, do your homework, perform on the cheerleading squad, and attempt to have a "normal" life. You live in a constant state of panic, never knowing when and where you'll black out again and start convulsing. Your peers whisper things behind your back, making high school harder than it already is, and it is difficult to make and keep friends. Most people don't like to hang out with someone who is your sort of "special." Your true friends show up, though, and if they are anything like my sweet Samantha, then you are a lucky little soul despite your misery.

So you cope.

It may take you weeks, months, or years, but eventually you will think it through and you will come to a conclusion. You will decide if you control what you can and cope with what you can't. You will live within the lines and boundaries only until you are strong enough to break them and reframe them. You will write your life one word at a time, each word being each breath that you take, knowing that everything can change in a heartbeat for better or for worse. But it doesn't matter, ultimately, because you are above your circumstances. You have a choice, every single day: What will you do with yourself? Will you allow your circumstances to shape you, or will you shape your circumstances? Will you be reactive or proactive? Will you be bitter, or will you be better?

You come to realize that the choice is yours.

16

PASTOR GRAYS

Sundays were busy. Our home was full of people—there must have been sixty or seventy at some point, with at least a sixth of them being family members—and most of them were crammed in the living room. They dressed in their Sunday best, sweating in the summer heat or shivering in the wintry cold. We didn't have the most spectacular amenities or insulation in our home. It had never been meant as a comfortable house of worship. But most of the folks didn't seem to mind. They had come to listen to words of wisdom. They had come to hear the pastor.

Pastor Grays.

I'm pretty sure you'd have recognized him if you were to have shown up to a Sunday service or to a Wednesday afternoon Bible study session, given all that I've shared with you to this point, but I doubt that you'd believe your eyes either.

Here's how it happened. When Sylvester Grays came back into our lives and tackled his third marriage to Evonne Grays in 1995, he continued to work as a security guard at St. Stephens for one more year. Then he quit and began a different job; he worked as a case manager at McAlister Institute, where he counseled recovering alcoholics. I found that madly ironic considering the fact that he was a recovering alcoholic himself—the kind who fell back into the bottle more times than he emerged from it. Not exactly a lead-by-example figurehead. Still, you had to give him his due. The man had charisma.

His next profession, however, took us even more by surprise.

One day he came home, set down his briefcase, and cleared his throat. My mother looked up from the stove where she was cooking fish. I was in a corner of the room, showing Laila how to plait her doll's hair into braids as we watched a show on TV with the rest of our siblings, waiting for dinner to be ready. The sunset flooded the room with gold-en-bronze rays that warmed and lulled us into a sense of security until my father broke the silence. He beamed at us all, his face filled with enthusiasm as if he was a proud Edward Rochester who was welcoming home his beloved Jane Eyre.

"I'm going to be a pastor," he announced.

Derrick and I looked at one other and then at my mother, dumb-founded. Our eyes asked each other: *What the hell?*

Apparently, becoming a pastor had always been on my dad's buck-et list. He had even gone to a ministry school two decades ago. Now, thanks to the encouragement of Sister Grace (who helped him set up the church, initially in our garage) and the realization that the friends he'd had in ministry school all had their own churches now, he decided that it was high time to fulfill his calling. *Maybe it's for the best,* the rest of the family thought. We told each other, *Maybe this means he's a changed man,* though I don't think anyone really believed that. You can only give a man so many chances. And if this wasn't ironic—the most lost man I've ever met, attempting to teach others how to find their way—then what was?

Mostly we were thinking: *Damn, this is random.*

He did it anyway. He launched Eternal Lighthouse Church when I was sixteen years old. A year later, he quit his job at McAlister in order to become a full-time pastor. Somewhere around this point, old Sister Grace up and died of a heart attack, leaving her champion to continue spreading the light himself. He ran the church for two more years until 1999. People came: family, neighbors, our dad's ex-colleagues, and the other strangers they brought along. The service lasted just an hour. It wasn't boring; given his way with words and his powers of persuasion, our dad was actually pretty good at it—at least as good as other such non-denominational Christian televangelists you've seen in the media.

At one point, he even tried to start a choir. Every Sunday my sisters and I had to dress up and come downstairs. We stood off to the side and tried to sing. He made us practice by listening to Gospel tapes and trying to sing along. Another member of the congregation tried to sing along and assist us. Nothing helped; we were terribly off-key.

This fiasco only lasted for a couple of months, probably because people's ears were bleeding. The whole situation irked me beyond belief, but it was often a point of comic relief for my siblings and me. As if it wasn't enough that we were forced to share our cramped space and give up our privacy to dozens of strangers, we had to dress up and perform tuneless spiritual sing-a-longs. It still makes me laugh when I wonder how all the windows and mirrors of our home didn't shatter at the sound of our yowling. The congregation was kind enough not to complain—at least not to our faces. Perhaps it helped that Dad served wine instead of the typical communion of grape juice.

Maybe it made the singing more bearable.

17

THE SILVER LINING

If I've learned one thing in this life, it's that there's always a silver lining. I didn't know it at the time, but my father's decision to become a pastor was exactly what I needed. His newfound calling meant that I was eligible for the pastor's child discount at a local private school: Point Loma Nazarene University, ranked among the top five most selective Christian colleges in the nation.

I wanted to go.

It seemed like a beautiful place, with iconic landmarks (including a Greek amphitheater and a large seaside athletic complex), tasteful architecture, and gorgeous Pacific Ocean views. The university seemed to focus on religion as much as on education, but I didn't think I would mind. I would be the first and only person in my family—to this day, at least—to get a college education, but that never fazed me.

I applied in 1998, writing an application essay—a story about the survival of the fittest—that was heartfelt and raw and maybe too close to home. I let my parents read it too, though I wondered how truthful or melodramatic they believed it to be. I sent it to the university. I got accepted.

...

Soon before I left, my mother gave my father an ultimatum: if he wanted to be a part of this family, he'd have to work to bring food to the table. He wasn't making enough money to support us as a pastor. Religion wasn't feeding us.

They began arguing more, too. At first they kept it behind closed doors, snarling at each other in the bedroom, but we kids could overhear them anyway. "You give the money you make to me!" he'd demand of her. "I am the man of this house!" Despite our mother being the steady breadwinner, our father always wanted to control the finances. I will never forget how, years ago, he'd stolen the cash given to me and Michael by the insurance company for our injuries after that fateful car crash. Instead of going toward our medicine and hospital examinations, the money (which was $2,500 in total, and supposed to go in a trust fund; our dad supposedly put $2,000 in the bank for us later—money which we never saw—and $500 in cash) vanished into thin air—probably air tainted with the ugly scent of alcohol. One day it had been on my dresser, the next day it hadn't, and my mom had seen my dad take it. Every penny I'd made since—by babysitting, by working at the zoo, by working anywhere—I'd hidden from my family, especially from him.

His insecure need to control the family, especially our mother, manifested in other ways, too. One rare day when my mom planned an outing for herself—she would be going skating with her sisters, and had told my dad about it in advance—he threw a fit when he saw her getting ready. She looked beautiful. He looked furious.

"Where are you going?" he demanded.

"I'm going skating with Di. I told you already."

"The hell you are!"

The argument lasted a while. Finally, deflated, my mother sat on the couch and held her head in her hands. My dad stormed to the bedroom and slammed the door behind him, believing he'd won the argument. I'd seen the whole thing play out. Frustration and resentment brewed in my heart as I watched my mom's crestfallen face.

"Mom, don't listen to him." She raised her head at the sound of my voice. I shook my head, exasperated. "Do what you want to do—go enjoy yourself, you deserve it! He can't control everything you do and expect you to be by his side every minute of the day. You are your own person! Go have fun."

My mom thought about it for a moment. Then she offered me a small smile and rose from the couch. "You're right." She grabbed her shoes, put them on, and opened the bedroom door to inform my dad: "I'm going, I'll see you later." Then she closed the door, took her purse, and left.

I think that's when my father realized that the whip he'd held over our mom's head was starting to fade. He was losing control. Shortly after, he began acting erratic again. And he began drinking on the low.

...

The demise of my parents' third marriage only confirmed that things wouldn't change if I didn't. This was a belief that I'd been cultivating inside me for a long time now, sheltering it among my other beliefs like a secret rose garden of truth, each flower beautiful yet painfully thorny. I couldn't wait for the story to shift; there were too many patterns in the narrative. I couldn't wait for people to change; a familiar path is always easier to follow. Only I could change my life. If I wanted to, I had the power to be the one responsible for my fate.

For *my way out.*

PLNU would be a place away from home, a place of opportunity, and a place of change. I yearned to experience life beyond this house and my family. All the people that I looked up to—from Chris Daniels to Mr. D. to Samantha to Oprah Winfrey—had attended college, and they often spoke about the importance of education.

I was ready. This was it. I was going to change my life.

I just had no idea how much crazier it could get.

PART 3
1998—2006

"IT ISN'T WHERE YOU COME FROM;
IT'S WHERE YOU'RE GOING THAT COUNTS."

—ELLA FITZGERALD

WOMAN OF SIN

A man showed up outside my apartment. He'd come to spend the night. We'd been dating five years, and I thought I was in love with him.

The night went by too fast, his kisses were hotter than burning wax, and I don't think either of us slept much. Before the sun had properly cleared the horizon, he'd shuffled out of bed and headed to the bathroom. I woke at the sound of the door opening and closing and heard the sound of streaming water as he turned on the shower faucet. I stretched around the sheets, wondering if I should sneak in a few more minutes of sleep before he had to get dressed for work and head out to the local T-Mobile store.

His phone trilled, shaking me out of my sleepy stupor. It wouldn't stop ringing. I stretched across the bed and picked it up from the night-stand where he'd set it along with his wallet. I froze when I saw the name that appeared across the flip phone's external screen.

SEXY.

I flipped the phone open. "Hello?"

"Hi," replied a woman's voice. Of course Sexy was a woman. "Is Jordan there?"

"Who is this?"

"It's his girlfriend."

I sat up on the bed, the sheets pooling around my lower body. "What?"

"His girlfriend."

"No," I said. "*I* am his girlfriend. I've been his girlfriend for five years."

"Are you sure?" She sounded a bit uncertain and, strangely, that calmed me. She didn't seem to be lying—or to believe she was lying. "He told me you had broken up. He said you couldn't accept it and you only showed up to his apartment a few nights ago because you were trying to get him back."

"No," I said again. I paused long enough to ensure that the shower was still audible and working behind the closed bathroom door. "That is definitely not what happened."

"Tell me your side of the story," she said.

So I did.

19

COLLEGE YEARS

Throughout my life, I'd had various ideas of what my vocation as an adult might be. As a kid, I was so influenced by Mr. Delgado and Chris Daniels that I'd often considered becoming a teacher or nurse. I played with the thought of acting too, but it wasn't a strong enough calling to propel me to Hollywood; deep down, I knew it wasn't my true passion, and I also sensed that actresses were largely dependent on others for their "lucky breaks."

I didn't want to be dependent on anybody.

I considered journalism for a while and signed up for a few internships at local networks. The excitement faded once I realized I didn't like the environment or the hours. I finally settled on being a Marketing major, feeling that "marketing" would be a future that could support me. Specifically, I chose Management and Organizational Communications, believing the broadness of the subject would allow me to tackle a variety of future professions.

My family had been neither overjoyed nor upset at seeing me off to college back in 1998. They were neutral about it, and I suppose I can't blame them. They certainly had their hands full regardless of whether or not I was around. Just as they'd never attended my high school cheerleading games, they didn't attend my college events either. I, of course, was elated at the opportunity to leave home. I moved in with an assigned roommate to an apartment hosted by Transitional Housing Continuum, a San Diego Youth and Community Services project. It promised "affordable housing, independent living skills training, and supportive training to create hope and self-sufficiency for youth transitioning into adulthood," and it delivered.

Unfortunately, it also delivered that roommate. I think she might have been discarded from the casting of *Carrie* or *Mean Girls*; like she'd been cast as an extra, one of those girls in the background glaring at the protagonist with a *you're-so-lame-and-unpopular-you-make-me-wanna-puke* face, but she'd been fired by the producers once they realized it was her real face and not an act.

Now she was my problem.

She wasn't enrolled in any college. She worked at a telemarketing center but was mostly shut in her room whenever I came home. I never missed her when she was gone; she was mean-spirited, lazy, and extremely sloppy, and we had nothing in common. One day I walked through the bright blue front door of our apartment to find her sitting in the living room, leafing through a gossip magazine and eating my food.

"Um, excuse me." I took off my shoes, fending off a jab of irritation by telling myself there must have been a misunderstanding. "Is that your food?"

She turned to glare at me and said, "It is now."

"Those are my things. I paid for them." It was too late to take them back now, as half of the lasagna was in her belly and the other half had her disgusting breath over it. "Why'd you do that? I respect your space and your things. You better never do this again."

"I'll do what I want." Her eyes appeared smaller and beadier than usual as she scrunched up her face. Food Stealer forked some more food into her mouth and flipped through her magazine. "You think 'cuz you're in school and have a job you're better than me, huh."

"I've never said or thought that."

"I'm sure you do. I think you think you're better. How come you act that way then, huh? You never want to even hang out with me."

The truth was, maybe I did try to steer clear of her. The case manager, who demanded mandatory sessions once a week, lived on-site and had permission to enter our apartment at any time to check if we were breaking any rules. She often showed up at our place after learning that my roommate brought over boys and frequently broke the no-sleepovers-allowed rule. It irked me that I was still dependent on a program and that someone could appear uninvited any time—and that my roommate gave her more incentive to do so—but it was a step closer to independence and it was only a ten-minute drive from the campus. I was busy, too. I worked full-time all throughout college—at the San Diego Urban League, as a nanny, and at the school library—and proudly afforded my own rent, car note, and groceries.

Groceries that had gone missing one too many times.

"You could *ask* me to hang out," I retorted, amazed that suddenly I was the bad guy in this conversation. "But you never have. You're always in your room and I'm gone most of the time. How am I supposed to know that bothered you? I'm not a mind-reader."

"Fine," Food Stealer sniffed. "Well, maybe it would be cool if we talked now and then, now that we're living together and all."

Sure, I thought.

I put a lock on my door the day after. I stored all of my things in my room from then on. Food Stealer never once asked me to hang out, and that was perfectly okay with me.

...

I suppose my college experience—what took place on the college campus, anyway—was ordinary enough. I lived away from home, studied, worked, got decent grades, learned new material, met many people, and graduated. Three months into living at the transitional living apartment, I found and moved into a one-bedroom apartment in the area, reveling in my personal space. I felt that I had a chance to spread my wings and fully reinvent myself. It took me longer to realize that, while I could run toward a brighter horizon, I couldn't run away from my past. Wherever I went, I took myself with me.

During my junior year, I decided to channel my inner Mary Poppins. I applied to an ad on a student job board at the college requesting a nanny and met a wonderful young couple who had just had an adorable baby girl. God knows I'd had enough experience caring for kids, so I felt capable enough. I was taking my medication and had the epilepsy under control; I hadn't had an episode for a year. Any qualms I may have had melted when they first placed that exquisite eight-week-old human in my arms. She scrunched up her button nose at me and flashed me a heart-stopping smile, showering me with love in the way of babies: unconditional, undeserved, undoing love. The parents offered me the position.

Of course I took the job.

I babysat a few times along with the infant's mother; she hadn't yet returned to work, first wanting to ensure that the baby and I grew familiar and comfortable with each other. One day, I headed straight to work, bone tired after an all-nighter of studying and an intense morning exam at the university. It was a new job and a good job; as tempting as it was to go home and get some much-needed sleep, I got in the car and headed to the couple's apartment.

You can't miss a day, I scolded myself. *You need the job. You love the job.*

So I showed up. It was a beautiful sunny day. I spent some time in the kitchen, chatting with the mother as she prepared some coffee.

"I think it's time for her nap," she said presently. She nodded toward the baby with a smile. "Would you like to take her up?"

"Of course!"

I scooped up the tiny human into my arms and headed upstairs, smiling as the baby cooed at me. My head spun with tiredness. I went through the motion of walking, my mind too tired to even worry about how I'd done on the exam. As I walked to the bedroom, a tremor jittered through my body as if I'd been jolted by a bit of electric voltage. A second rattling jolt—this one of terror—immediately followed. Panicking, I sprinted to the crib as quickly as I could. My hands managed to hold on to the baby long enough to lay her down safely.

And then: darkness.

I woke up in the hospital a while later. A doctor loomed over my bed, explaining his clinical version of the story. My mother's worried eyes stared at me from where she perched on the chair next to me. She clasped my hand. "It's okay," she said. "You're fine. The baby's fine. Nobody got hurt."

There was that, at least. But it wasn't enough. Shame pulsed through me, flaming my cheeks and stinging my eyes. "You don't understand," I gasped, haunted by the horror of what could have happened. "I almost dropped her. I could have hurt her badly. It would have all been my fault."

But I hadn't, and it wasn't. The parents, unbelievably, still wanted me to nanny their infant. Their trust and generosity warmed my heart, but I couldn't accept the position. Putting myself in their shoes, I knew I'd never feel completely at ease with someone like me watching over a helpless baby, knowing there was a very slim but not inconceivable chance that something would trigger another seizure.

As it was, the seizure ensured that I had extra complications to deal with; upon learning of it, the DMV revoked my driver's license for six months, as was mandatory. I used the bus to get to and from my apartment and the campus, feeling frustrated at lost time and at this backward step that had me depending on others to pick me up and take me places where and when I couldn't take the bus. My clipped wings also meant that I wasn't free to pursue the jobs that I wanted, and I had to realign the balance between my health and my schoolwork. In the six months that it took for me to regain my license, I opted for student loans to help me pay my rent and utilities.

Regaining my license? Highlight of the year.

Above all, it's hard to look back on those college years because they will forever be shadowed by two off-campus relationships that I cultivated: one with a man and one with a church.

Point Loma Nazarene University (PLNU for short) was a gorgeously situated campus with thoughtfully organized classes, enchanting seaside views, and a decent student body. My first year taught me that the college experience is something that can often extend far beyond the campus. If I hadn't gone to PLNU, I'd never have met Ella. If I'd never met Ella, I'd never have attended Devout Life in Jesus Church. That's where my worldview shifted. That's where, years later, a flat-screen TV nearly killed my cousin's six-year-old daughter.

And that's where I met Jordan.

20

THE CHURCH AND THE HUSTLER

For about four years, I was a devout follower of Devout Life in Jesus Church.

It began with a yearning to confess. On my fourth visit to the church with Ella, the pastor announced an Altar Call at the end of the evangelical address, calling on anyone who desired to confess. "I beseech you therefore, brethren," he bellowed at the room, his voice seeping into the cracks of the walls and of our lonely hearts, "by the mercies of God, that you present your bodies a living sacrifice, holy, acceptable unto God, which is your reasonable service..." The congregation belted out a lively hymn, clapping as a few people approached the altar to be "saved." The church stirred to life around me, every face animated and participating, a sight I'd never seen so fully before in any house of worship.

Heart pattering, swept up in a strange tempest of emotions, I found myself rising from my seat and stepping toward the front of the church. The pastor beamed at me as I approached. His cries rebounded from the rafters to the floor beams: *Pray for healing! Rededicate your soul and give in not to the lapse of religion in your life! Surrender to God! Ask for His blessing!*

Along with dozens of others, I knelt on the floor and bowed my head, clasping my hands together and letting my emotions wash through me.

I'd always been Christian, but I'd avoided going to church since my parents' third divorce. They'd called it quits soon after I was accepted to Point Loma, the summer after my high school graduation. I'd retaliated by partying and dating—basically sinning against God, according to these parishioners. The guilt of that—and, perhaps more so, a desire to find solace somewhere—had me walking up to the altar and asking for a confession.

Thus I joined the church.

It was different from the one on campus. PLNU's Brown Chapel had never felt like a choice. I hadn't gotten used to being herded to mandatory chapel services. All students had to attend services twice a week—services during which all classes paused and it was as if time froze on campus—and walk through the heavy doors of Brown Chapel after scanning their ID. The requirement bit into my skin like a leash that tugged against my sense of liberation. I did it because I had to.

Devout Life in Jesus Church felt different.

Partially, I suppose, it was because attending services there felt like my choice. I had Ella to thank, too. We'd met during the second semester of freshman year in 1999; we were the only two black girls in the Communications Department that year. She'd found me studying on the sunny lawn outside the Greek amphitheater one afternoon and introduced herself, winning me over with her genuine smile and sweet spirit. Her dark chocolate skin seemed to glow in the sunshine, and her voice was firm but friendly. We struck up a conversation and found out that we had a few mutual acquaintances from our high school and neighborhoods. We both felt driven to make something of ourselves, but we also shared a mutual love of reading, journalism, music, and getting girly by pampering our nails and hair. It was comforting to find a friendly face on campus, given that none of my older friends attended PLNU. A few weeks into our friendship, Ella invited me to join her at a Devout Life in Jesus Church service.

It wasn't anything to brag about, not back then. It didn't even look like a church yet. Given a limited budget, the founders of Devout Life in Jesus Church had congregated in a small business park building. It originally boasted no more than fifty members—fewer than the folks who showed up to my father's services in our living room (and later on at an actual church building) not that long ago. Yet here, the sense of community warmed me. The solidarity fulfilled me. You were "one of us" when you were there. Everything was all right. Every Sunday's Celebration Service filled my heart with its heartfelt cries of *Hallelujah* and *Glory be to God*, with the nods and smiles and *Amen!*s of the congregation that felt more familiar and familial as the days and weeks and months trickled by.

But all was not all right.

...

I bumped into a young man at the church one day on the way out. Or maybe he bumped into me. What I remember is that he was tall, dark, and handsome like the heroes of the romance novels that I secretly adored so much. His teeth were white as pearls, his skin as dark and sweet as a chocolate Hershey's Kiss, and he smelled of cologne and fresh soap. He sported a fade haircut with a trendy hairline trim. He was smartly dressed and had the kind smile of a man who hasn't lost the last of his boyhood innocence.

"Excuse me," he said. I nearly jumped out of my skin at the thrill when he touched my arm in apology.

"Jordan," Ella said, grinning at the both of us. "You haven't met my new friend Constance yet, have you?"

Jordan flashed a brilliant smile at me. "Not officially, I'm afraid."

"Jordan is Ethan's roommate." Ella held onto my arm, fending off the people who jostled us as they bustled out of the building now that the service was done. I smiled. Ethan was Ella's boyfriend. Given the good nature of that couple, I couldn't help but warm to Jordan immediately. "Hey, Ethan and I are going out to lunch now." She winked at me. "I was going to ask you anyway. Jordan, feel like joining us?"

"Sure." Jordan offered me his arm, the perfect gentleman. I took it with a cocked eyebrow that I hoped would hide my pleasure under a veil of amusement. By the time we'd reached the restaurant, I knew that he was from Chicago and had grown up with his mother—a single working mom—his sister, and his niece. When we were seated at a table, I sat next to Ella; Jordan and Ethan sat across from us. Ella struck up a conversation with Ethan, keeping him occupied as long as Jordan spoke to me.

"I enlisted to get away from Chicago." Jordan leaned across the table toward me to keep his voice low. "I think a lot of guys in my shoes do the same. We go to escape."

"I can understand that. My older brother joined the Navy about a year ago."

I still missed Derrick fiercely. He'd had a horrific argument with our dad right before I'd left for college. It began with a fight between Derrick and Michael, which our father had broken up by seizing Derrick and pushing him against the wall. *Get your hands off me,* Derrick spat out, tears of rage brightening his eyes. *Who do you think you are? You're not my dad, Sylvester! Let me go!* I witnessed the scene, my own eyes wet with frustration and hurt as I tried to talk them out of it. Our dad finally let go, and Derrick bolted to his room. He stayed in there for a while, packing his bags. Finally eighteen, Derrick had the power to escape by enlisting. So he left, secretly and silently, in the middle of the night and without a goodbye. It had been two months before he'd shown signs of life. He contacted our mom after he finished his basic training and told her that he'd joined the Navy. Part of me was proud of him and happy for his escape; part of me felt left behind, lonely, and even betrayed by the fact of his absence. Now he was stationed in Atlanta. I'd heard he'd just gotten married and had a daughter. He'd moved on and made a new family; I felt like a ghost of his past.

I sighed, bringing my attention back to Jordan. "What brought you to San Diego, then?"

"It's as good a place as any other to be. I got stationed here for work, but I like everything I've seen so far." He smiled shyly. "I can think of something that could potentially keep me here."

Oh, he was good.

I hadn't woken up that morning imagining I'd be having lunch with a handsome electrician who was fresh out of the military. How could I have guessed that, not even an hour after the church's service had ended, I'd be sharing a plate of French fries with an interesting man who didn't know exactly what he wanted to do with the rest of his life, who was enamored with my own backstory and my drive to make something of myself? He found me beautiful and brave and sassy, and asked for my phone number to call me "sometime."

He called me that very night.

Jordan wasn't my first crush, but he became my first love. I'd lost my virginity during my senior year of high school to a young man who'd asked me out after my shift as a waitress at Ruby's Restaurant. Ruby's was at the local mall; my uniform consisted of a striped dress and a white cap, and I was still wearing it on the night he first asked me out. Derrick had interrogated him when he'd found out about him. The young man passed the test, apparently, because I started introducing him as my boyfriend. The first time we had sex, it was awkward and unfulfilling, and that was probably more my fault than his. His hands undressed and caressed my body, but I could barely feel them beneath the haze of guilt that enshrouded me. My mother's warnings of shame and blasphemy haunted me; I wept with guilt as soon as I realized we'd crossed the line, convinced that I was defying God and losing a part of myself. My teary reaction freaked him out. We continued to see each other halfheartedly for about another week or two until I stopped returning his calls and ended things, feeling ashamed and dirty.

With Jordan, though, it felt different. I'd become more comfortable with myself and my sexuality. Even though I'd rekindled a connection to God and felt pressured to act based on a moral compass, I sensed that my value as a person probably wasn't based on who I chose to kiss or sleep with. As long as I wasn't hurting anyone or intentionally breaking hearts, what was so wrong about falling in love?

I was sure that our pastor could give a very lengthy lecture detailing the full extent of why and how it was so horrifically wrong…but I didn't really want to think about that. And with Jordan, I usually didn't have to. When we were together, I could barely think of anything.

Days flowed into weeks, dates morphed into decisions. Before long, Jordan opened my eyes to the rose-tinted world of young love and budding romance. This world is a garden—one that feels secretive and specially tailored to everyone who stumbles upon it, though nearly all of us do at least once in our lives—bursting with blushing roses, red and rosy and seductive, all petals and no thorns, all tingling kisses and confiding whispers and gentle caresses in the dead of night.

Resistance doesn't come easily in a magical realm like that.

We stole hours from each other's days and found that they sped by like seconds. We knew we were pushing boundaries and crossing lines, but it was just too hard to resist. Deep at my core, I never *wanted* to resist. What evil could there be in love? We both sensed that each kiss and caress was taking us closer and closer to the inevitable point when our clothes would come off and we'd be pressed against one another's flesh…and we couldn't help ourselves. Yes, my conscience ate at me. Jordan's conscience ate at him, too. Everything we were doing pulled us farther from the path that our church and the Bible sought to teach us.

But it's true what they say: forbidden fruit is the sweetest.

Jordan may have been an electrician, but I later discovered that he was, at heart, a hustler. He worked for a few years at a T-Mobile store. I was furious and upset once I found him doing shady part-time work, pocketing the money that he made by stealing and selling phones. He didn't stop, though he promised to. And despite his shortcomings, I could not disbelieve the authenticity of his compassion toward me, his gentility, and his charm.

THE PASTOR'S RULES

Jordan sat in his car outside my apartment, the motor of the vehicle still running. I could see him through the window, waiting for me. I was ready. I was stalling.

This is dumb. I took a deep breath and smoothed my hair and my dress. *But whatever. We go, we talk, we leave. How bad could it get?*

I left the apartment and followed the walkway. When I reached the car, I got in without greeting Jordan. He didn't say anything either, even though the appointment was his idea; he just started the car. We exchanged one look and he drove on in silence.

There's a reason we're doing this. It's fine. I glanced again at Jordan, suddenly nervous. *Ella and Ethan confessed. We should too; that's why. I suppose everybody else would, in our shoes. It's the right thing to do.*

The silence broke my heart. I reached over and touched Jordan's fist as it rested on the gearshift knob. He didn't look away from the road, but his palm opened to accept mine and he interlaced my fingers with his. Jordan was the opposite of just about every guy I'd met until the day I met him. He was a gentleman; he opened doors for me, paid on every date, listened to me when I spoke, and wanted to spend time with me. Despite his good looks and trendy haircut—he'd been blessed with dark chocolatey skin, pearly white teeth, and the body of a basketball player—he had an aura of kindness and innocence that labeled him, in my eyes, as a good, God-fearing man.

That's why we're doing this, I reminded myself. *He has good intentions and he loves me.*

We arrived at the building that served as our church—it could easily be mistaken for a warehouse—and waited silently in the lobby. I closed my eyes and drank in the comforting scent of Jordan: cologne and fresh soap. Someone finally came and informed us the pastor was available to see us.

The pastor looked up when we entered the room. He gestured to the uncomfortable chairs situated across from his desk. "Have a seat, my children." He studied our faces, his own face grim and unwelcoming as if he already knew what we had come to say. A feeling of dread trickled down my spine like a spilled glass of cold water. "How can I help you? What would you like to discuss with me today?"

"Pastor." Jordan cleared his throat. "Forgive us. We've sinned and have come to ask forgiveness. We've done something God wouldn't want us doing."

"What have you done?"

"We have..." Jordan glanced at me. I fought to keep my face expressionless. "We've been having sex."

The pastor scrunched up his pudgy face as if a sour lemon had just been shoved into his mouth. His brow furrowed, and new angles structured his face into a mask of anger. "Well," he said. "That's not good." His eyebrows rose at an afterthought. "You aren't a married couple, I assume?"

"No," Jordan confirmed.

The eyebrows lowered and clenched as the pastor frowned.

"God does not like sinners," the pastor informed us, wagging a finger at us and blinding me momentarily with the golden nugget that cuffed his shirtsleeve. "Because of your mistake, you will no longer date. I want you to separate yourself from each other—"

"What?" I exclaimed.

"—for a minimum of six months." He glared at me for interrupting him. "Spend that time with God and cleanse yourselves of your sin. You are also barred from working in the church during this time. Jordan, you will no longer be allowed to volunteer with the Youth Ministry. Constance, you will no longer be working in the Children's Ministry. It's such a shame, too, because you know how much our church suffers and needs volunteers who are devoted to God. You are not the type of example we want working with the kids."

He sat up straighter behind his magnificent desk, squaring his short shoulders beneath his expensive suit. I didn't have to glance behind the desk to know that his shoes were impeccably polished. I didn't have to gaze out the window to remember that the gleaming Jaguar in the parking lot was his.

Example? I raged internally. *Who are you, really, to speak to me of example?*

"After six months, we will meet again and discuss your time apart. We'll see if you have grown. If I feel you can date again after your time apart, we will have that conversation. Spend this time with God, pray for forgiveness, and work out your salvation."

Jordan and I stared at each other, dumbstruck.

"Do you understand me?" the pastor rumbled.

"Yes, Pastor," we said.

"Great." His fleshy face softened, and he gave us a triumphant smile. "Have a good afternoon and I'll see you Sunday. God bless you."

...

We rose from our seats when the pastor dismissed us and headed outside toward the car without a word. We didn't hold hands. Jordan opened the passenger's door for me and I ducked into the seat, unable even to look at him.

The tears began rolling down my cheeks once we pulled onto my street.

Jordan's face tightened with distress as he parked the car. "It's going to be okay, Constance." His promise fell flat on my ears, as lifeless and heavy as one of the paperweights in the pastor's office. "We can get through this together."

"We can't do it *together*," I retorted. "That was his whole point." My fists clenched of their own accord. I stared ahead at the windshield in front of me as my tears transformed it into a blurry Van Gogh painting of blue sky and gray asphalt and budding trees. "Who is he to tell us what we can and cannot do? He's not our parents and we are not children! We can do what we want."

"No, we can't. We have to do what the pastor said." Jordan reached out to stroke my hair as he tried to make eye contact with me. "Hey, relax! I don't want to stop seeing you. I love you. What's so bad about waiting six months? I'm not going to change my mind about us. I don't think that what we did is so bad that we have to separate."

My heart dropped at the sound of his voice siding with the ridiculous rules of a patriarchal dissembler.

He reached over and hugged me. "I know this is going to be hard, but it's the right thing to do. We'll still be together after six months."

"So you're telling me you really want to do this?"

"Yes."

I felt as if Jordan had suddenly yanked the car seat from right under my body and had me sprawling on the pavement beneath the car, upending our relationship when I thought it was at its strongest. We had talked about getting engaged, we'd daydreamed about how married life could be...and now this was it? We were a modern-day Romeo and Juliet torn apart by a hypocritical mouthpiece of God, and here was a

Romeo who couldn't even care less. I extracted myself from his arms, opened the door on my side of the car, and stepped out.

I walked away without saying goodbye.

22

WOLVES IN SHEEP'S CLOTHING

The thing that irks me most is that I should have known better. Maya Angelou is quoted to have said: "When people show you who they are, believe them the first time." But I hadn't. I'd quenched my doubts and quelled my fears in a treacherous yearning to belong, to be free to make my own choices, to be loved, to be different and better and stronger and to seek a role model who apparently could show me how.

For a long while, I looked up to the pastor. He spoke like a car salesman, with a deep and persuasive voice, and could have been considered charismatic if you hadn't met my father. I initially respected him based on his sermons and the way that he and his wife—they actually referred to her as the First Lady, as if he was the nation's president—carried themselves. They'd met at a home Bible study in 1980s Japan and described themselves as family-oriented. Above all, they seemed like a fierce power couple, and I admired that. Someday, I wanted to *be* that.

I'm an all-or-nothing sort of girl; I decided I wouldn't be a halfway Christian. I'd given up cussing, listening to secular music, hanging out with non-Christians, and spending time with friends or family members who didn't seem to believe as much as I did. Until I met Jordan, I'd been fiercely abstinent, feeling too intimidated to even date. I invited every single person in my family to go to church with me and would often drop by the house to pick up my siblings and let them carpool with me. Aunt Ledesi and Sanaa began attending church as devoutly as I did.

As time went by, I could no longer ignore the fact that something felt off.

What I heard and what I saw did not always seem in tandem. Some things that were supposed to run in parallel seemed to career off-track and crash into perpendiculars. "Be humble!" roared a pastor who bedecked himself and his wife in gold chains and jewels. "Feed the poor!" he demanded of us, fueling his car after the service with the 10 percent tithes and offerings he received. "Give your wealth to God and He will provide for your financial freedom, just as He has cared for me!" he advised, raking in cash that helped him afford ever-more-expensive suits and cars and cruises that he shamelessly bragged about. "Bless me and my wife," he'd ask, neglecting to pray for the poorer members of the church. "Pray for our salvation."

It reminded me of that old fable I'd come across years ago, the one with those baby goats that waited at home for their mother to return. A wolf had arrived and eventually tricked them into opening the door by bundling himself in stolen sheep's fleece. The baby goats opened the door and the wolf devoured them. Upon her arrival, the mother goat saved her kids by cutting open the wolf's belly while he slept, freeing the goats and filling the wolf's insides with rocks before stitching him back up and shoving him into a lake. We don't all have goat mothers (or fairy goat godmothers) looking after us, however. When the wolf devours us, we have to rip a way out of its belly ourselves.

Otherwise, we'll be stuck in that darkness forever.

...

An ever-growing sensation of wrongness in my heart and my gut eventually compelled me to leave the church. Most predominantly, I felt ever more uneasy at the greediness and unethical nature exuding from the pastor, which felt unquestioned by the cult he'd created. Devout Life in Jesus Church had a "Creflo Dollar" mentality, believing in prosperity theology: that faith, positive speech, and (especially!) monetary donations to religious causes increase a person's material wealth. In other words, the Bible is a sort of financial contract between God and mankind: if we have faith in Him, He will deliver security and prosperity. While some aspects of this sort of preaching may be beneficial—promoting personal empowerment, for example, and a positive outlook—it is very easy for this sort of practice to become exploitative, irresponsible, and contrary to scripture.

The church felt judgmental, too. I was not perfect, but didn't scripture say let he who has not sinned cast the first stone? Where was the love? Where was the forgiveness? The pastor's ego inflated as he received more money, more groveling, more flattery—and it seemed as if people never stopped to question how purely he served as a mouthpiece of God. The church should have been a sanctuary, a place free of bias and hate and trickery. Yet I would leave services feeling dirty and guilty, a modern-day Jezebel. I would feel used and voiceless. I felt estranged from my relationship, my family, and my core values.

The pastor led by example, and his disciples followed. I saw many situations that echoed his unethical behavior and that went unnoticed or unpunished. One of the scariest scenarios happened after I'd left the church. Sanaa had been attending church and had left her six-year-old daughter at the church daycare. A little boy accidentally knocked a huge TV onto Sanaa's daughter's head, cracking her skull. The kids had been left unattended and nobody was quick enough to intercept the accident. Someone heard kids screaming; the little girl was rushed to the hospital.

To add insult to injury, the church rejected all responsibility and refused to pay for any of the hospital bills. Sanaa furiously sued the church and won the case in court. Many people sided with the church. Unsettlingly, Sanaa's own mother—compassionate, logical, wonderful Aunt Ledesi—wrote an open letter in support of the church's stance, siding with the pastor over her daughter. That in and of itself—striking against my face like a red flag showing how much a cult really could brainwash a person—chilled me to the bone. I believe it would have snapped me out of my own daze if I hadn't woken to the truth already.

The final straw for me, though, was the pastor's rule forbidding me to see Jordan. I left the cult in 2002 and never set foot there again. Many churchgoers turned their backs on me in turn, refusing to speak or interact with me after I refused to show up, believing me blasphemous. Even Ella turned away for a time, causing a rift in our friendship that never fully healed. But I reconstructed the bridges I'd broken with my family and old friends.

A month after I'd left, Jordan showed up at my doorstep, pledging that he couldn't spend another day without me. We picked up where we'd left off; Jordan lived a double life, confessing nothing of what we did to the pastor. It took him another year and a half to leave the church.

...

I graduated with the PLNU Class of 2003, walking across the auditorium's stage and accepting my diploma in Management and Organizational Communications with indescribable pride. I'd done it, balancing my studies and work and student loans and random roommates and greedy church cults and new friendships and a difficult relationship. The memory of that day is a happy blur in my mind, but I remember accepting the delicate scroll of paper and feeling an overwhelming rush of emotion, recognizing all the past, present, and future elements of my life that this degree embodied.

My family attended, rooting for me in the bleachers of the auditorium in which the graduation ceremony was held, knowing that I was the first Grays in my immediate family to go and graduate from college. My mom and siblings showered me with flowers, and my Aunt Ledesi took plenty of pictures. Sylvester Grays didn't show up, of course, just as he hadn't shown up for four long years and would continue to not show up for a long while still. Nobody expected him to.

"Show us around the campus," my mom encouraged me after the ceremony. She and my Aunt Ledesi walked around with me, taking more pictures and enjoying the beautiful day. My siblings and friends vanished—"to beat the traffic home," my mom explained. I shrugged and figured that I'd find time to hang out with them over the summer anyway.

I had no idea that everyone had scurried away to Uncle Kahari's house to get things ready. For the first time in my life, my mother threw a surprise graduation party for me later at his house with the rest of the family, covering the walls with banners and balloons, showing up with a gorgeous cake and startling me to tears. My siblings and friends were there, and Jordan was too. I remember looking around at everyone and feeling a lightness in my chest that I hadn't felt in a long while.

I felt happy.

My college experience taught me that I had the potential to make it on my own. I couldn't and wouldn't bite away a helping hand, but I knew I had the grit to win my independence in the long run. I continued experimenting with jobs and housing after graduation. I left my apartment and moved in with Aunt Ledesi for a couple months until I secured a new job at San Diego Gas and Electric sifting through a mountain of paperwork and data entry. It wasn't my dream job (and I wasn't quite sure yet what that dream job would be, exactly), but it paid the bills and helped me get back on my feet. With a bit of cash in hand, I moved into my second apartment, and—with Samantha's mom's help—secured a great deal on a new black Mustang after my old car left me in the dirt.

23

THE OTHER WOMAN

Jordan had been busy, too. He'd started working at Ethan's janitorial business a while back. They worked at night, made some cash, and then started a habit of partying the rest of the night away to blow off steam. More than once, my room reeked of alcohol when Jordan crashed at my apartment some mornings and slumped into my bed before I had to head to work. His heavy drinking worried me, but he reassured me it wasn't frequent or that heavy. He never staggered home to me completely drunk.

For the last week, however, he had been evading my calls for two days straight. Worried and frustrated, I'd driven to his apartment and knocked on the door. Ethan had answered, explaining that Jordan wasn't home and no, he didn't know when his roommate would be back. I thanked Ethan, stormed back to my car, and waited in the parking lot. Now that I knew Jordan hadn't been killed or abducted in the past forty-eight hours, my worry hardened to anger.

Nearly an hour later, a brand-new blue Mercedes pulled up the street and parked a little farther away from Jordan's apartment—far away enough that the visitor wouldn't know exactly which one his apartment was, but not far away enough hide from my line of sight. The door on the driver's side opened. Jordan stepped out. The woman who had been sitting next to him slinked into the driver's seat. He bent down and kissed her through the open window. They exchanged a few words I couldn't hear.

Words I didn't need to hear.

I lunged out of my car and slammed the door shut. My Mustang rollicked at the impact, but I had no sympathy to spare for my hard-earned car. It didn't compare to her Mercedes. Jordan's head swiveled toward my direction at the sound. He froze like a deer in the head-lights.

"Who the fuck is this?" I demanded, walking up to them. "So now you're cheating on me? How dare you? Who is this bitch, does she know you have a girlfriend?" I turned to the woman in the driver's seat. Her bewildered face stared back at me. "What are you doing? He has a girlfriend and you're fucking him!"

Jordan tried to touch me, but I backed away. He held his hands out as if to placate a kid having a tantrum. "It's not what you think, Constance. She's just my friend. Nothing happened, okay?"

The woman in the car stared at him incredulously. "Oh okay," she snapped. "I see how it is." Then she looked at me and shook her head. "I didn't know he had a girlfriend." Before either of us could reply, she'd revved up the Mercedes and drove around and away from us.

"You were with her?" I tried to fight back the tears as sorrow reared its sad blue head to stand alongside my red rage. "After all we've been through? I've supported you, I've loved you…" There had been times in our relationship when Jordan had been broke, when he'd come begging to me for help. I'd bought him food and essentials. I'd stocked up his apartment more than once. He'd just been using me. It wasn't just about lost love—it was about integrity. It was about showing respect for a fellow human being. The betrayal overwhelmed me. "And this is how you treat me?"

"Constance—Constance, wait…It's not like that…"

I couldn't stand his sniveling lies. I shook my head and stormed back to my car. He followed me, standing in front of my car now, leaning forward so that his hands splayed on the hood.

"Get out of the way," I demanded. "*Now.*"

An eerie echo whispered through my mind. A flashback of my father leaving my mother, telling her to *get out of the way* because he wanted to leave. Except I hadn't stolen a car, and I wasn't the one betraying and abandoning a relationship. I glared at Jordan. "Get. Out. of. The way."

Jordan jumped out of the way when I started driving, realizing that I'd hit him if he did not move. He watched me go. Or maybe he didn't. I don't know.

He wasn't worth watching in the rear mirror.

…

A few days later, Jordan showed up at my door, begging forgiveness and asking me to remember all that we'd been through. I missed him; I relented. Not even a week later, I picked up Jordan's ringing phone from the nightstand as he showered that morning in my apartment and answered: "Hello?"

"Hi," replied a woman's voice. "Is Jordan there?"

And that was Seiko.

"Who is this?"

"It's his girlfriend."

"What?"

"His girlfriend."

"No. *I* am his girlfriend. I've been his girlfriend for five years."

"Are you sure? He told me you had broken up. He said you couldn't accept it and you only showed up to his apartment a few nights ago because you were trying to get him back."

"No. That is definitely not what happened."

"Tell me your side of the story," she said.

I could hear earnestness in Seiko's voice. Authenticity. Shock. She couldn't fake her distress any more than I could fake mine. And so I found myself explaining the truth as our mutual player continued to soap himself up. "I caught him lying to me again last week," I concluded. "Then *he* showed up at *my* door to beg for another chance."

In light of all that, Seiko's call didn't come as the most earth-shattering surprise. In the span of our brief conversation, we realized this man had managed to dupe both of us. Hustling wasn't his profession; it was his purpose for existing.

"You know what?" Seiko gave a grim laugh. "How about we go out and show him? You come downtown with me. We can have dinner and go out and party."

It felt surreal, but I'd been in stranger situations. "Sounds fun. Why not? He deserves it." I gave her my number; a moment later, my phone beeped with a text so I had her number, too.

The bathroom door opened, and Jordan appeared with a smug smile on his face and a towel wrapped around his waist. The smile evaporated like vapor when he saw the look on my face as I ended the call on his phone.

"Who is that?" he demanded. "Who are you talking to?"

"You know Seiko?"

He lunged at me, trying to grab away the phone.

"It's too late for that." I threw the phone across the room. "She isn't going to see you anymore. In fact, we'll be hanging out tonight." I rose from the bed and clenched my hands into fists to keep them from shaking. "Get out of my house, you lying, cheating loser."

Disbelief flitted over his face, sparring with outrage and guilt. "What?"

"GET OUT!"

"Hang on—" He stumbled comically around the room as he

struggled to pull on his underwear as fast as he could. "Woman, I need my clothes."

"Do I look like I give a damn about your clothes?" I picked up my phone. "Get the hell out of my house RIGHT NOW or I'm calling the police."

Jordan growled and grabbed his pants on his way to the door. In his wake, he discarded the towel, his dignity, and five years' worth of pleasure and pain. I threw his shirt and shoes out the window. His footsteps faded from the room, and the brightness of the morning sun faded with them.

24

FLYING FREE

I'd met Seiko under ugly circumstances as "the other woman"—which was how she'd thought of me, too—but I came to really like and admire her the more I got to know her. At least five years older than me, Seiko was a trailblazing entrepreneur in her field who'd launched and branded some of the city's most spectacular nightclubs. Doll-like with her small stature and lush curves, you could easily forget that this little beauty was a fierce CEO with connections everywhere; with a snap of her fingers or a wink, she could ensure that we got into any club that we desired, never had to wait in line, enjoyed all the VIP events, and received drinks and food for free.

It was like partying with a genie; I'd wished *let me get over Jordan*, and she'd materialized fun, festivity, alcohol, and handsome people to blur the pain of the past. I began drinking—tentatively at first, because I'd always held back due to religion and a fear of recurring epilepsy, then more liberally once I found that it didn't bother me—and dating again. I continued working at the San Diego Gas and Electric Company and moved out of my one-bedroom apartment in Linda Vista to an adorable apartment in Chula Vista. I lived for the weekends, when I'd sleep in the day and party long into the night. We dressed up like Furtado, Fergie, and the Pussycat Dolls and mimicked their moves from our favorite music videos. My objective was to have fun, and I did.

Breaking up with my college sweetheart taught me that I had to think for myself, that I deserved respect, and I had a right to *demand* it. If a person really loves you, he or she will never cheat on you. I know that now. At that point in time, though, all I wanted to do was numb the pain and feel free. I needed to get over him.

I only saw Jordan once, a few weeks after the breakup. Seiko and I had decided to hit up a new club downtown that night. I'd just downed my second vodka and headed out to the dance floor to groove with some new friends in a crowd of smiling faces, all of us jostling and grinding together to the month's hottest new tracks. He materialized in that sea of people, his smiling face in smacking distance from mine.

"Hey, Constance," he said. The music lulled at that moment, easily carrying his voice to my ears.

The smile froze on my face. I felt as if someone had doused me with a bucket of cold water. The nerve of him! I watched him coldly, unable or unwilling to reply. He'd been calling me repeatedly; while I refused to pick up, my heart clenched every time I saw his name on the phone screen.

Suddenly Seiko appeared next to me. She gave him a scathing look and, without a word, pulled my hand and led me deeper into the sea of dancing bodies as the music amped up again.

"Fuck him," she yelled at me, her voice barely audible over the song. "It's his loss. We don't need him! Have a good time and show him what he's missing out on!"

We linked hands for a while and our bodies undulated to the beat. I closed my eyes and let the rhythm wash over me, sweeping away the memories and the freshly opened wound caused by Jordan's voice and gaze. I remembered how angry and bitter I felt against him. When I opened my eyes again, Seiko had somehow steered us into the arms of two cute guys who were more than happy to dance with us. I saw Jordan watching, and I let my dance partner flirt with me. When I glanced again toward where Jordan had been standing, he'd disappeared. Seiko smiled back at me triumphantly.

And I knew I'd be fine.

...

When my mother was in the first grade, she couldn't see the board due to poor eyesight. When the teacher asked her a question, my mother couldn't answer. She was too afraid to admit that she needed glasses and could not see what was written on the board. The teacher strode over, yanked Evonne out of her chair, and shook her until her little shoes fell off. "You're stupid!" the teacher reprimanded her over and over in front of the entire class. "Stupid!"

When my grandmother learned of this, she visited the school and informed the teacher that if she ever touched Evonne again, my grandmother would kill her. In retaliation, the teacher flunked my mother, forcing her to repeat the first grade. When my grandfather learned of this, he was disgusted with his daughter. "Evonne, you're dumb," he said, echoing the horrible message of the teacher. "You should wear the Dumb Girl hat." Evonne grew up in a tornado of household violence, mental abuse, and molestation by her older brother, a cycle of horrors that haunted her and sank her into bouts of dark depression. As a girl, she'd wanted to be a nurse like her mother; these dreams were dashed by an early pregnancy and a pattern of abusive relationships. Does it really come as a surprise that dysfunctionality lured her? It was the only thing she really knew.

Sometimes I think that Evonne's nine children represented nine attempts at unconditional love, nine shots at hope, nine tries to prove herself as being good, as being lovable, as being enough. It tears me to the bone when I think about that. I hope that we have helped her, to whatever possible degree, and that we've added more beauty than burden to her life after all.

When my dad left us for the third and final time, my mother continued working at McAlister Institute and moved back into a cramped apartment to make ends meet. I can only imagine her shame and embarrassment as she ended up the fool once again, duped for a third time by Sylvester. The third time they'd married, I suspect it was more a plea for help than a plea for love, but even this sort of plea fell on deaf ears. My dad disappeared and she was "dumb Evonne" all over again.

My sisters say that she withdrew into herself completely in her attempt to deal with everything that had happened; obviously, she had neither the means nor the time to seek therapy. She barely had the time or the energy to have a real conversation with my siblings for a year. I dropped by the house occasionally, leaving behind some money whenever I had savings. I took my younger sisters out to lunch, and I remember helping with their clothing and hair before their dances and proms, but I wasn't around as much as I used to be. In retrospect, it's evident to me that I ran, just as Derrick had run, driven by an instinctive need to get away from a broken family and a shitty apartment in a bad ghetto. I did not take into account my sisters' point of view. I didn't realize that they missed me as much as I missed Derrick, and my absence felt as much a betrayal to them as his absence felt to me. I'd been their second mom, practically raising them, and suddenly I was nearly as absent as our dad. Absorbed in my own life and struggles, I failed to notice and thus failed to care.

After I graduated, my mom moved into a bigger house in a better neighborhood with a friend, and they opened up a daycare center together. Things improved in the years that followed; my sisters did better in school and my mom seemed happier. The hurts of the past began to heal. That's how it goes, that's what they say: time heals all wounds.

The scars remain, of course, as lifelong reminders. They show where you've been. But they don't need to determine where you'll go.

...

By my twenty-sixth birthday, each of my siblings had chosen their own path. Mia had become more stable, stopped smoking, and lived in a halfway home. Andre had fallen off my radar, but I heard he'd moved to L.A. with aspirations of becoming an actor. Derrick got married and now lived in Atlanta with his wife and daughter. Michael moved to Oakland and became a father, working different odd jobs as he tried to break into the music industry as a rapper. Alyssa and Laila were working at a hotel, and Xavier dabbled in insurance. Jeremiah, between hustling and getting into trouble, managed to charm a lovely paralegal named Natalie and had two kids before she ended the relationship, fed up with his philandering and abusive tendencies.

As for me? I was doing just fine.

As I grew up, so did my friendships. Though I hung out a lot with Seiko, Samantha and I reconnected after I graduated and broke away from the circles I'd developed both with Jordan and with the church. A year older, Samantha had already gotten her degree in Human Resources from SDSU and now lived at the new apartment community in Chula Vista. She only paid a small amount of rent because she was fostering a baby girl and thus qualified for low-income housing. At one point, she suggested that I move in with her so that I could save money. I accepted gladly, looking forward to her company and knowing it would slash my rent by half. Steadfast and sweet: that'd always been Samantha to a T.

Ella turned her back on me when I left the church as if I'd committed some sort of sin and she'd be deemed guilty by association. She moved away shortly thereafter, and I didn't hear from her for years. Ironically enough, she found herself in my shoes when she eventually moved on from the church and her boyfriend, too. At some point she even reached out to me again, hoping to reconnect, but I had moved on. I'd learned to not give second chances lightly.

Apart from Seiko and Samantha, two rays of sunshine and hope in my life at the time included my dear friends Damion and Natalie. I'd known Damion since high school, and we'd even dated briefly during senior year. We realized that we were better off as friends and fortunately we remained close; in the years that followed, I found myself blessed and grateful to have such a good person to count on and have fun with. Damion was dependable and kind, the sort of person you could do and say anything with. We went to the movies together, talked about people we were dating, and kept each other company at barbecues and parties. When I got a DUI one night during a tipsy escapade on the freeway with Seiko, Damion was the one who picked me up from jail. I met Natalie once she started dating Jeremiah. Everyone in the family adored her for being sweet, funny, smart, and reliable. While their relationship didn't last, our friendship did; I love her like a sister to this day.

2006 was a good year for me, a time of freedom and independence. I embraced my femininity and sensuality and youth, realizing that young adulthood had its merits. For the first time in my life, I felt I could truly let loose. I didn't worry about religion, I didn't have a boyfriend to hold me down, and I didn't have my family around to impose a curfew or extra responsibilities on me. I could do what I wanted, date who I desired, and live as I chose without being judged or restricted.

For a time, I was free.

PART 4
2006—2010

"YOU MAY ENCOUNTER MANY DEFEATS, BUT YOU MUST NOT BE DEFEAT-
ED. IN FACT, IT MAY BE NECESSARY TO ENCOUNTER THE DEFEATS, SO YOU
CAN KNOW WHO YOU ARE, WHAT YOU CAN RISE FROM, HOW YOU CAN
STILL COME OUT OF IT."

—MAYA ANGELOU

25

Not My Type

One November weekend night in 2006, I escaped the chill of the weather and the world by slipping into the sultry darkness of one of my favorite nightclubs. Night Lounge's name was innocuous and the club it-self was small, with no blatant reference to the darkly magical, seductive, and luxurious atmosphere that hid within. In the heart of the Gaslamp District, it was upscale casual, a treasure trove of leather booths, velvet couches, erotic paintings, birdcages, and ambient lighting. The true pulse of the place was its people, of course; dolled up and with a face gilded in makeup, I felt as fearless and sophisticated as the best of them.

When I walked in, the DJ's eyes pierced mine.

I'd met him earlier that evening at another club where Seiko and I had been having drinks. He was tall and skinny, with a shock of dirty blond hair, a quick smile, and soft blue eyes. He walked by us, lugging his DJ equipment along with the help of one of his friends, and flashed us a big grin. Then his eyes seemed to drink me in within the span of a heartbeat, taking in the sheen of my flat-ironed inky hair cascading down my back, the tightness of my crop top and my jeans, the way I stood my ground in my favorite heels. His eyes crinkled, liking what they saw; his was the sort of stare that made you feel desirable, not dirty—a good man's stare.

"Who's your friend?" he asked Seiko. His eyes didn't leave mine. I couldn't help it; I smiled back.

"This is Constance," Seiko said.

"Hello," I added.

"Hello!" He grinned. "I don't think I've seen you around before. Where'd you two meet up?"

"MeetaHotChick.com," Seiko joked. It was her go-to quip whenever people asked how we'd met. It suited me just fine and it was the perfect ice-breaker.

The DJ laughed. "I'm Nathan." He rearranged his grip around the equipment so he wouldn't drop it and glanced at his friend. The friend took the cue and the remainder of the equipment and kept walking. "I've got twenty minutes before I've got to get this music blasting. Can I buy you ladies another drink?"

Within those twenty minutes, I learned that Nathan was a professional DJ from L.A. who played hip-hop music at Night Lounge. "That's where I know you!" I exclaimed. We'd met before—Seiko had actually introduced us at his club one night—but Nathan had gotten distracted with the equipment and I'd quickly drifted away with Seiko.

"That's right. And I swore to myself if I saw you again, I'd come talk to you." He stood up as his watch beeped, signaling that his time was up. "I've got to run, ladies. You should come by the club to see me later tonight."

We smiled and waved him away. When he disappeared into the crowd, Seiko turned to face me with a crooked smile and a cocked eyebrow. "He likes you."

"What?"

"He asked me to introduce you to him. I told him we'd be here and he came and found us. He doesn't do that often."

"Um…" My cheeks felt warm. "He's not really my type."

"He's cute and a good guy." Seiko shrugged. "Why not test it and see? Got nothing to lose, right?"

I supposed that I didn't. So later that night, Seiko and I ended up at Night Lounge; she ensured that we got VIP service and a good view of the DJ. He saw us come in and winked at me. Transitioning to another song bought him enough time to come over and greet us, saying he hoped we'd stay awhile. An hour later, he invited me up to the DJ booth to hang out for a bit before the music lured me down to the dance floor again. A few songs later, caught up in the fervor of drinking and dancing, I made it back to his booth.

Why not? I heard Seiko's voice echo in my head. *Nothing to lose…* The alcohol and vibe of the club loosened my inhibitions. When Nathan turned with a smile to welcome me back, I kissed him.

His eyes widened. His eyebrows rose as if trying to shape themselves into question marks. But he kissed me back, his hot mouth crushing against mine, and now he smiled.

"I wanted to know if there was chemistry," I said.

"Was there?"

"Maybe." I walked away, biting my lip to keep from grinning.

26

FOOL'S GOLD

There's something uniquely beautiful about the holiday season, an aura of festivity and fun and universal goodwill that affects people. While there are plenty of Scrooge- or Grinch-like characters year-round who don't cut some slack even during "the most wonderful time of the year," most of us are infected by seasonal cheer and optimism. We notice the homeless a little bit more. We donate to the Red Cross and the Salvation Army. We get presents for people we like and sometimes for people we don't really like as much. We dare to dream of a better coming year.

This season is characterized by its decorations and colors: crisp green trees and gorgeous red ribbons, vibrant wrapping paper and glistening ornaments. We're surrounded by golden lights, golden baubles, golden hopes, and the golden romances of Hallmark holiday movies. Maybe this blinds us. Maybe we forget to be wary. Maybe we fail to recognize fool's gold when we see it.

A couple of days later, Nathan picked me up from the apartment I shared with Samantha and took me out to the Old Town Mexican Café, rumored to have the best handmade tortillas in the region. Old Town is gorgeous and quaint throughout the year; during the holiday season, it's an even cozier neighborhood, brimming with Christmas trees and garlands and bright wreaths and festive lights. As we waited to be seated, we watched the brawny, white-aproned women working their magic right inside the front window, pummeling and kneading and whirling around their tortillas.

Nathan leaned against the glass and grinned at me. "So, you're from San Diego? Your family is based here, too?"

"Born and raised here." I offered him a crooked smile. "I've got eight siblings. You're looking at Number Four."

"Wow! Big family. I've just got a sister. She's a few years younger."

"That sounds nice." I watched the women bustling around their kitchen, their flowing dialogue muffled by the glass window, their movements precise and swift and coordinated. "We were so many, it was pure and utter chaos."

"Never a dull moment, at least…?"

I laughed. "Yeah, you can definitely say that."

The door opened and we were ushered into the restaurant. The food was worth the wait; the tortillas were as delicious and piping hot as they'd been advertised to be. Nathan and I finally got to talk to each other without yelling over music or getting distracted by spontaneous champagne showers on the dance floor. Between sipping a refill of his Coke and asking for the check, he asked if I'd decorated for Christmas yet.

"I haven't gotten around to buying a tree yet." I shrugged. "My roommate Samantha has one and it's small and cute, but you can barely call it a family tree. There's only room for so many ornaments, you know? So I'm not sure that decorating is on my Christmas list this year."

"Christmas isn't the same if you don't decorate a tree." He gasped, mock-serious. "You can't have Christmas without a huge fresh tree, woman!"

"Sorry, Santa." I laughed and leaned across the table to gently punch his shoulder. Nathan guffawed and then made a funny face as he pretended to stagger from the impact, glass of Coke in hand, and almost spilled his drink on the table. "Maybe I'll hang up a stocking or something. Have you decorated yet?"

"I'm Jewish," he said, that teasing grin still on his face. "But I'm not the Grinch or anything. Of course I've decorated."

After dinner, as if to counter the spiciness with a good dose of sweetness, Nathan prolonged the date by treating me to ice cream as we ambled around Old Town's streets and headed to the nearby park. The lingering sunrays and Christmas decorations burgeoning in the windows of the storefronts warmed me as much as Nathan's hand around mine; the earth's carpet of crisp brown leaves and the bronze haze of a cloud-speckled sunset reminded us of winter's onset.

"I was really excited for our date tonight," he confessed. "Ever since I first saw you, I knew I wanted to get to know you better. I was curious about you. I still am."

The night of that first kiss a couple of days ago, he'd walked Seiko and me back to our cars when the party was over. He'd asked for my phone number, called me, and reminisced about the kiss. *Maybe I was too direct,* I'd said over the phone. *Your directness was very sexy,* he'd countered. I glanced at him now, wondering for a moment how far this spontaneous journey could go, wondering if a white Jewish boy was actually a disguised knight in shining armor, wondering if we might end up playing for keeps. Why not? Stranger things had happened in my life. Hope pulsed through me and filled me with warmth. For now, I felt good and desirable, and I knew that these weren't emotions that you pushed aside so easily.

"The first time was a very brief meeting," I reminded him.

"Doesn't matter." He paused and reached over to tuck a strand of hair behind my ear. "It doesn't have to take forever to realize you want to get to know someone. You're real beautiful, you know."

My cheeks warmed at the compliment. "Thank you…" I stuck

out my tongue and rolled my eyes while making goofy faces as I tried to keep from blushing harder. "Is it all you thought it would be?"

He laughed. "Even better than I'd expected."

...

He was sweet, that was the thing. If you were to have asked me, I would have told you nope, no thanks, dating a white Jewish DJ wasn't exactly my thing—but then again, why did I have to have a thing? Most importantly, what did I have to lose? It wasn't love at first sight, but his kindness and attention won me over. With his lean build, bright blue eyes, shock of brown-blond hair, and easygoing smile, he could certainly be considered handsome. Best of all, he liked me.

A couple of days later, the doorbell rang at Samantha's apartment. She left me eating dinner with little Sarah at the kitchen table and went to answer. I watched her walk to the door, certain that it was her darling boyfriend, and I felt a tinge of sadness. Once upon a time, we'd been that excited to see each other, running upstairs to her room or mine to talk about boys and listen to a new CD by Destiny's Child or Lauryn Hill. Samantha and I had grown distant lately. It hadn't been purposeful and it wasn't as if we'd fought over anything. We still cared about each other. One time I had a tremor at the apartment—the closest I'd come to an epileptic fit during those years—and had cut my thumb to the bone while chopping vegetables for dinner; Samantha rushed me to the hospital so I could get stitches. But as the months went by, it was almost as if we'd outgrown living together. Our lifestyles meant that we were rarely at home at the same time. Even when we were, it felt like neither of us had much to say that the other person would find interesting.

Once Samantha reached the door, I didn't hear her usual squeal of delight. I headed out of the kitchen just as she turned her head to look at me with a cocked eyebrow. "Connie?" she said. "I'm pretty sure this is for you."

I came to the door to find Nathan on the doorstep, grinning beneath his lopsided hat and hugging a Christmas tree.

27

TRUTH AND TEAR

"Have you thought this through?"

"Yeah." I smiled at Samantha. "It's what I want."

She frowned, crossing her arms across her chest in a way that was becoming annoyingly habitual. "I don't think it's a good idea."

"It *is* a good idea." The reasons flitted through my head—reasons I didn't say out loud and some that I didn't even consciously realize at the time. *Because he likes me. Because I like him. Because you have a boyfriend who has practically moved in with you and is so ready to have me move out. Because you're raising a little girl and, between the three of you, there's no space for me in here anymore. Because I need to get out. Because I don't want to be alone.*

"You barely know him," she said. "You've known him like, what, two months? Was this his idea?"

"I know him well enough. And yes, for the record, it *was* his idea." I'd been planning to move out for a while, feeling an uneasy mix of claustrophobia and disconnection. During one evening spent at Nathan's place, where I'd been staying more and more frequently, he'd seen me hunting through apartment ads. *What's this?* he asked. *You're looking for a new place?* When I explained how things were getting crowded at Samantha's, Nathan sat down next to me and wrapped an arm around my shoulder. *Well, why don't you just stay with me? And if you want to move out to another apartment, you can just keep looking while you're here.* Well, why not? I couldn't see why Samantha disapproved. "Thank you for your opinion and all," I added, "but please do me a favor and let's face the fact that it's time for me to move out of here."

"Fine." Samantha shook her head, exasperated. "Do *me* a favor, okay? Take that dumb Christmas tree with you—or throw it away, I don't care. And you still owe the last month of rent."

It hurt, as the truth tends to hurt. When Samantha expressed her disapproval of Nathan, we were way beyond our days of bonding over crushes and heartbreaks. We'd become distant, cordial roommates. Her concern and her questions should have unsettled me; caught in a trap of emotion and circumstance, I brushed them aside like unwanted cobwebs.

She tried to warn me, still.

...

In the ensuing months, Nathan and I basked in the warmth and romance characteristic of most new relationships. A couple weeks after Nathan invited me to move in with him, as I was still apartment hunting, he asked me to stay for good. I did. I also met his family when they flew in to visit us from L.A. and quickly fell in love with his parents and sister. He met my family too, who decided they really liked him because I really liked him and he was a cool guy. Everyone was getting along marvelously.

Well, almost everyone.

In the beginning, we all tend to overlook the little things, rarely pinpointing which of those are actually the big things. I told myself that it didn't bother me that Nathan was out of the house some nights all night. I told myself it didn't bother me that he played music as exotic dancers performed erotically on the stage nearby. I told myself that it didn't matter that he smoked weed, because lots of folks in nightlife did and he would outgrow it soon enough. He was trying to make an honest living, was trying to cope with his own inner demons, and was going to want to change because he loved me.

One afternoon, a year and a half into the relationship, I called Nathan from the apartment after a trip to the local pharmacy.

"Nathan?" I fought to stay calm as my voice caught in my throat. "Oh my God, oh my God…"

"What? Constance?" His voice sharpened with concern. "What is it?"

For a strange second, I recalled a popular game which my siblings and I used to play as children: Truth or Dare. I felt, for just a moment, as if Nathan and I were playing this game, but this time my choice between the truth and the dare was one and the same: *I dare you to be the ultimate adult…and that's the naked truth.*

"I'm pregnant."

"What?" I could almost hear his jaw drop. "Whoa…how did that happen? I thought we were on birth control. What about your patch?"

"We are." I bit my lip, jittery with conflicting emotions. "I guess there's always a percentage of times that it doesn't work. And with my medication, maybe…" While I only suspected it at the time, we found it to be true: the medication I took for epilepsy nulled the effects of the birth control.

"Ah…um, okay. I'll be home soon, sweetie, so we can talk about it later, okay?" I heard noises on the other end of the line, as if he'd dropped a piece of equipment or something. "But wow…"

Later that evening, hearts pounding and thoughts whirling, we talked. This wasn't something we'd planned, let alone considered. We weren't even married. On the other hand, the thought of an abortion was like a stab in the gut. I couldn't give up a little soul—children were miracles, God's creations—and it just didn't feel right. But having a kid with Nathan? Was *that* right?

"What do you think?" I asked him. "I don't know how this would work…"

A little voice in my head asked a familiar question: *Have you thought this through?*

I tried to shrug that voice away. *Yeah. It's what I want.*

I don't think it's a good idea, the little voice warned.

Then Nathan said, "I want us to keep it. And that's the truth!"

"Really?"

"It'll work—we'll make it work." His blue eyes sparkled as he held my hands. "Let's do it! We'll have our little boy…or our little girl… our baby would be so cute, Constance. I'm excited! This is awesome!" He started kissing me until I laughed and kissed him back. The tension in my chest dissolved. "I'm going to call my parents and tell them our news!"

…

Nathan's parents visited once or twice a month from L.A. Sometimes we met up in Vegas, their favorite place to vacation. They always had something small and generous to surprise us with, whether it was presents for an expected baby, toys for our two dogs, or ornaments for our Christmas tree. Most importantly, they gifted me time, taking me out to lunch or shopping, talking to me, sharing afternoons with me, treating me like a real daughter. They spent time getting to know my mother and siblings, making an effort to unite our families, and I loved them for their compassion and thoughtfulness. They supported my efforts as I tried to wean Nathan off the drugs and excessive nightlife, warning him that it wasn't healthy for a father-to-be.

Soon after we realized we were going to have a baby together, I gave Nathan an ultimatum. I'd been watching shows and reading books, particularly one that counseled: *Why buy the cow when you can get the milk for free?* The author's relationship advice haunted me, building on the engrained belief that I *had* to be married by the time I was thirty years old. I'd recently attended other friends' weddings, including Samantha's. Though I probably wouldn't or couldn't have told you at the time, it was my underlying, burning, secret desire: I wanted the white picket fence, the soulmate, and the happy family I'd never had and had always dreamed about. Nathan and I had been together almost two years. I was twenty-eight. When I realized I was pregnant, I followed in the footsteps of my mother, bowing down to the pressures of society and my pattering heart; and so, I pressured Nathan.

"I can't go on like this. This isn't respectful, you know. Are you serious about me or not? If you don't marry me," I warned him, "we're over. We're either creating a family or we're not."

"We're...what?" He laughed uneasily and tried to shrug it off as a joke. His face fell when he realized that I wasn't joking. "Constance, of course I'm serious about you."

He did his best to live up to those words. One afternoon, he drove me out to Sunset Cliffs, a paradise of dramatic cliff formations and breathtaking panoramic views. Predictably, we reached the perfect spot well before dusk. With the backdrop of an incredible blood-red sunset that set the sky on fire and the applause of the crashing waves barreling against the rocks below, Nathan got down on one knee.

He presented me with a ring—one that we'd gone shopping for together a few days before—and asked me to marry him. He didn't do it because something in his heart warned him that he couldn't live without me. He did it because he liked living with me but mostly because I'd demanded it. I know this now.

The wind whipped through my hair and whooshed past my ears, asking: *Have you thought this through?* The dying sunrays pierced my eyes, blinding me momentarily as if reminding me: *It's what you want, isn't it?*

I thought I'd be emotional when Nathan proposed to me. I wasn't. I simply said *yes.*

...

Several weeks later, we went to the doctor for our first ultrasound, grinning ear-to-ear and holding hands. I was eight weeks pregnant. We'd told our folks and were warmed by their obvious joy. Nathan's mother couldn't help herself; she told me she'd already begun buying baby clothes.

After conducting the necessary examination, the doctor sat us down in his office and informed us that the baby had no heartbeat.

I felt like he'd put on a pair of boxing gloves and knocked the wind out of me, bruising my heart in the process. Nathan and I stared into each other's eyes, speechless. The rest of the dialogue faded in my ears. Our baby would never see the light of day. I was carrying a dead fetus inside me. I wept all the way home.

"Don't worry about it," Nathan comforted me. "It could happen to anyone, truly. We'll try again."

We did. We loved the excitement that we'd felt when we'd been expecting, and we were still young, still in love, still optimistic. We had our whole lives in front of us. We adopted two beautiful dogs: an adorable Maltese named Diamond and a feisty Mini Schnauzer named Jerome. In the process, I made a new best friend: Jasmine, who sold me Diamond. Jasmine was kind, warm, and thoughtful—traits that made her shine as a friend as well as a pediatric nurse—and we shared a love of dogs, North Park walks, and good conversation, so we enjoyed many girl dates together. Nathan and I sometimes went on double dates with her and her fiancé, Logan.

Six months later—and two years into the relationship—I found myself pregnant again.

This time, we decided, things would be different. We were engaged, soon to be married. Apart from his DJ gigs, Nathan worked at the family upholstery business and made a decent income. We'd moved into a beautiful, brand-new, high-rise loft downtown despite my arguments against the purchase (I'd gotten a job at the Home Buyer's Guide, spending my days visiting new home communities and talking to real estate agents, and I knew the housing market wasn't doing well). I'd been visiting both of my neurologists and a high-risk specialist who assured me I was nice and healthy and shouldn't have a problem getting and carrying a baby. I'd also been reading about epilepsy and infertility; even though there could be a number of complications, it appeared a high percentage of epileptic women still managed to have healthy babies. This time, we waited a few more weeks before telling our families that I was pregnant again, just to be on the safe side.

The thing was, there was no safe side.

The second pregnancy also ended in miscarriage. No heartbeat. No baby.

Shame and sorrow enveloped me like a shroud, suffocating me. Where had I gone wrong? Wasn't having epilepsy bad enough? Why was my body turning against me?

Shortly after I lost my second baby, my younger sister Alyssa announced to our family that she was pregnant. Conflicting emotions raged through me, threatening to tear me apart. She was my sweet little sister, and I wanted nothing more than to wholeheartedly rejoice for her. As the weeks trickled by and her belly grew and grew, I bought her gifts and often cooked for her. When she delivered her baby, I called her to express my congratulations. I couldn't bring myself to visit them at the hospital and meet my niece, however. I couldn't bear to see them. I felt like a failure: childless, alone, and worthless. I was envious of their joy and guilty for feeling that way. I knew that I should have been full-heartedly happy for her…and I couldn't be.

Nathan did his best to comfort me, and I did my best to comfort Nathan. We started attending therapy together—we used our pregnancy problems as the official reason for attendance, but I was mostly driven there by my frustration with our sexless marriage. Both of us felt but could not confess the underlying truth: this second miscarriage was a very heavy straw on a relationship that was fragile to begin with.

I didn't want to wait for a natural miscarriage, so I went under the knife and had my second D&C ("dilation and curettage"), which scraped my uterus to clean the lining, thinning it and building up more scar tissue. Again the news tore a hole in my heart. Again the knife tore through my body. Nathan's parents had gifted us with a vintage white rocking chair that used to rock Nathan to sleep. One day, I pushed that chair, motionless and hauntingly empty, into a dark corner of our home. I piled blankets and boxes on it, turning it into a makeshift shelf. I ignored it until I pretended I'd forgotten about it.

But no matter how hard you try to ignore it, the truth doesn't disappear. It waits in the corner, patient as the universe. And when the time comes, it will rear its head and face you.

28

BAD OMENS

On my wedding day, I cried as I shaved my legs in the bathroom of the hotel room. Natalie arrived to help me get ready; I didn't hear her come in and looked up to find her staring at me from the doorway with a stricken look on her face. I must have looked pretty out of place, my tears falling on the expensive porcelain and cloud-soft towels of the gorgeous Venetian in Vegas, our wedding venue.

"Constance, are you all right?" She rushed over and embraced me, wiping away my tears. "You're shaking…"

Nathan's father had suffered a heart attack the night before. We'd spent all morning at the hospital, returning to the hotel just two hours before the ceremony. We couldn't call it off; my soon-to-be father-in-law was stable, and my whole family had traveled to Vegas for the wedding. I hadn't eaten all day. I couldn't even stomach a full glass of champagne. I was exhausted, sad, and scared.

It shouldn't be like this, I thought, telling Natalie that it was just the stress from the hospital. *Isn't my wedding day supposed to be the happiest day of my life?*

The road to our marriage was flanked by red flags. I ignored some and misunderstood others. Some flags cropped up before I walked down the aisle in a white satin dress. One waved at me during the wedding ceremony, reflected in the redness of Nathan's stoned eyes. Even more popped up after. It didn't matter. You don't know which way to run when you find yourself blindfolded in the middle of a bull pen.

I suppose I had dangerous role models. My grandmother and grandfather were high school sweethearts. Theirs began as a young and innocent love which took a dark and nearly deadly turn for the worse. Back in the day, men would get away with beating their wives (and the saying "throwing hot grits on him" illustrates one of the few ways a woman could get a man to stop abusing her). In their apartment complex, my mother once heard a neighbor screaming for help as her husband hit her; she pleaded with my grandfather to go help. "That's their business, and we mind our own," he told her. Right before my grandmother decided to flee with her kids, she stabbed my grandfather during a fight, literally fighting for her life. Life smiled a bit on her after she retired from nursing at age fifty. That's when she met and married dear dependable old Jim; though they divorced fifteen years later (my grandmother prized her independence more than anything), I always sensed that he continued loving her.

My mother met her first husband when she was a high schooler, too. She was already pregnant with Mia on the day of high school graduation. Though she's said she never loved her first husband, she felt pressured to marry him due to the pregnancy. His addiction to drugs obliterated any hopes of them having a normal family life, however; my mother left him shortly after giving birth to their second child, Andre. She later met my father at church, kind of like how I met Jordan. If only she'd had a crystal ball to see what was to come.

Because we already know how that played out.

A few weeks prior, I'd flown up to Vegas to do a tasting at the hotel venue for the wedding with Nathan's mom. She'd asked me, "Are you sure you want this, Constance? You sure you want to marry Nathan?" I thought it was a strange question, but I couldn't doubt the authenticity in her voice and the kindness in her eyes. I knew how she felt about me—in retrospect, her concern for me would show it even more. I told her I was absolutely sure I wanted to marry her son. "Okay," she said, embracing me. "Just want to make sure you're sure…" It was as if she knew something I didn't know—or knew but didn't want to admit. Everything in this relationship had happened so quickly, so suddenly, so impulsively…and Nathan's mom, like Samantha, was trying to look out for me, echoing the familiar question: *Have you thought this through?*

I thought I wanted Nathan. I didn't want to admit that I'd become more and more secretive of our crumbling relationship. I was ashamed to share that we weren't the picture-perfect couple that our families and friends thought we were. My mom enjoyed cooking for Nathan and laughed at his jokes, my sisters thought he was nice, and my brothers liked him because he got high with them. My mother believed I was doing so much better than she'd been at my age, so she was happy for me.

Now I rushed to get ready with Natalie, becoming even more upset at having to rush. I barely had time to take a shower and get dressed before Nathan and his groomsmen showed up at the door with the photographer so we could have our pre-ceremony pictures taken. Half an hour later, I swallowed my nerves and my distress and pasted a big smile on my face as my mother walked me down the aisle. Nathan seemed nervous and scared during the ceremony; his voice grew shaky when he spoke his vows and he said that he was sad that his dad wasn't there. After our traditional first dance at the venue, his eyes seemed more glassy than usual. He'd been smoking something for sure, on this day of all days.

The "best day of my life" ended with me on a bed somewhere apart from Nathan, staring at the golden wedding band on my finger. Gold is cold if it is not warmed by another person holding your hand.

Nathan got so high and drunk at the reception that at one point he disappeared altogether. We didn't sleep together on our wedding night. Nathan stumbled into the hotel bridal suite with a stoned friend sometime before dawn. He'd crashed on the bed while his friend sprawled on the couch.

I was mad but I forgave him, as usual, making excuses for him even when he didn't have the guts to make them up himself: *He was sad his dad wasn't at the wedding. He felt pressured and couldn't cope with being in the spotlight. He had never considered himself the "marrying type" so, if you thought about it, it was sort of sweet that he would propose and marry me after all. He was having a last bout of fun before the duties of married life molded him into a more responsible character.*

Nathan was fool's gold and I was a fool, believing that I could change another person by sheer will.

...

Nathan's drug addiction began to bother me more; I tried to initiate sex but Nathan was usually too stoned to last for a minute or more. He often turned me down, even when I wore his favorite lingerie, and I couldn't understand why he didn't desire me anymore.

"What the hell is the matter with you?" I exploded one night after yet another rejection, tired of sleeping in a bed with a man who treated me as if I was invisible. I was fed up with curling up to sleep without even an arm around me, without a kiss on my lips, without the heat of a loving body pressed against mine. I sat up in the bed and yanked the covers away from my husband. "What is *wrong* with you? What is wrong with *me*?"

Nathan flinched at my outburst, his reaction time just a bit delayed by his intoxication. "Take it easy," he mumbled. "You can't sleep?"

"You want to *sleep*?" In a spurt of rage, I imagined tearing the blanket and sheets and pillows and yanking them to the floor, pushing him off the bed along with them. Feeling heartbroken and foolish, I rose from the bed and stripped off my sensual slip, pulling on warm pajamas instead. "Seriously, nothing else? You don't find me attractive, not even a little bit?"

Nathan stared at me, red-eyed and smelling faintly of marijuana. I couldn't read his expression. His initial liveliness from an afternoon of rolling cigarettes had dissipated into lethargy. In our earliest days together, this man hadn't been able to keep his hands off of me, praising my hour-glass figure, full lips, and rounded breasts. Now I saw myself as an utter stranger in his half-lidded eyes.

"We're going to a therapist," I told him, getting back into bed and turning my back on him. "Or I'll leave and you'll never see me again."

He fell asleep before I did.

...

I'm not sure how much the therapy actually helped. He kept blaming it on the weed, repeating, "It's not her, it's me." Nathan promised that he'd stop smoking—if he did, he claimed, then that would change his sexual desire. Also, he was busy working late, and was "just tired" when he got home late. Sex "wasn't a priority" when you were that tired. After months of therapy and no signs of change, the therapist advised us to call off the wedding and break up.

I should have listened. It was obvious Nathan didn't want to change and wouldn't. Continuing therapy was useless. He just wanted me around as his trophy wife, a pretty face that he could parade around to show that he was "successfully" married. Nobody knew the real truth except us and the therapist—and only the therapist had the right attitude.

Instead, I decided that the therapist didn't know what she was talking about. She didn't realize that Nathan and I had really loved each other and that everything would be okay once we had a kid. Nathan would be more affectionate and would desire me again, he'd want to stay home with me more often, and we'd have something—a real family—to bond over. I was a visionary and a hard worker; I'd work hard and make this work. We *did* get married, and I got pregnant for a third time, six months later. The news lifted our spirits and warmed our hearts for a while. We waited for twelve painstaking weeks. When we saw the baby's heartbeat and got our ultrasound pictures, Nathan and I were ecstatic. This time, I told my entire family, emboldened by my joy and my conviction that everything would be okay.

Nathan's parents came down to San Diego to visit us during the Christmas holidays. Nathan and his production company threw lavish parties for New Year's Eve at hotel venues, so his mother and I went to the mall together to shop for a dress a few days before the event. Nathan's dad came with us, doing some Christmas shopping of his own. At twelve weeks, I wasn't showing much and I was excited to attend the party.

Heat and dizziness overwhelmed me suddenly as I browsed through a rack of dresses. I looked down and saw blood running down my leg beneath my skirt. I passed out. Nathan's parents carried me out and rushed me to the hospital as I bled all over the backseat of their car.

I woke up on a bed in the emergency room with Nathan by my side. His hands clenched mine. He had tears in his eyes. When I met his eyes and he saw I was awake, those tears trickled down his face and he kissed my hand. In that moment, at least, he truly loved me.

I'd hemorrhaged so much that I almost needed a blood transfusion. Once I became fully lucid and the pain medication subsided, Nathan's parents burst into the room and hugged me, telling me how afraid they'd been and how relieved they were now that I was okay. In the darkness of my pain and sadness, their love was a ray of sunshine and hope.

But there would be no baby.

29

BROKEN

Like my mother, I tried desperately to believe that the way to patch up a troubled relationship was by having a baby, despite having a legacy of examples that showed otherwise. After the third miscarriage, however, I fell into a deep depression. I couldn't sleep, wouldn't eat, and felt stressed and miserable. My world had fallen apart. My life trickled along without purpose or passion, leaving me helpless and unhappy.

As if God enjoyed adding insult to injury, my dear friend Jasmine announced her pregnancy after I lost my baby. She'd been going through fertility treatments and ultimately found herself carrying twins. When she invited me to her ultrasound for the gender reveal four months in, I couldn't refuse her. I gazed at the monitor where the fetuses appeared, their hearts beating steadily. One of the boys was sucking his thumb while the other one wiggled around to gain more room. I held Jasmine's hand and told her how happy I was to experience this with her as the doctor moved the ultrasound machine over her belly.

When I drove away from the hospital, tears spilled down my cheeks. "Why?" I whispered. "Why are You allowing everyone to have their children while I keep losing mine?" My knuckles turned white as I clenched the steering wheel. I should have known by then that reproaching God wouldn't really make a difference.

When Jasmine gave birth to her twins a few weeks early, I went to see her. She let me hold them. I did so with a sense of awe, cradling their tiny bodies in my arms. They were so heartbreakingly beautiful. I was proud of myself for having the strength to at least show up. Their presence softened the blow, somehow, and my heart filled with joy for Jasmine. As I left, however, I couldn't shake off a gaping feeling of emptiness. I couldn't reconcile with God. Jasmine was such a healthy and happy mother—and she deserved nothing less.

But would it ever be my turn?

Shortly after, I had my first tonic-clonic seizure in over three years. In all that time, I'd just had a rare little tremor here or there, which abated with medicine and a good night's sleep. Nathan witnessed it all: how I fell and writhed on the floor, how my limbs twitched and tightened up like a zombie's, how I couldn't control my bowel movements, how I woke up sobbing uncontrollably, how I completely and totally lost myself. He rushed me to the hospital, nearly as helpless and as terrified as I was. The seizures continued; Nathan called for an ambulance whenever I didn't come back to my senses quickly enough.

I'd lost more weight, hope, and joy with every miscarriage. Our sexless marriage was going down the drain, the medical bills were piling up, and the loft was undergoing foreclosure. The upholstery business had slowed, Nathan worked more night gigs that paid less, and my epilepsy and hospital stints forced me to take a break from work. Not only did I have student loans to pay, but leaving my job meant I didn't have insurance all the time; Nathan covered me with his insurance, being self-employed, but it was expensive. He continued smoking weed and we continued attending therapy in an attempt to salvage what was left of our relationship.

Doctors began tweaking my medicine again. They still couldn't explain why all the pregnancies had ended in miscarriages—maybe the medication, maybe just bad luck. They blamed recurring epilepsy on the stress. "Are you stressed?" the doctors and nurses asked me. "Any recent traumas in your life that may have upset your body?"

"Yes," I told them. "That might be why."

...

During the last week of January, on the night of his birthday, Nathan didn't come home. I called him repeatedly and he didn't answer. At 1 a.m., he finally picked up the phone.

"Hey, Constance…"

"Nathan, what's going on?" I demanded, worry sparring with fury. "Are you okay?"

"Fine," he slurred. "I'm tired. And drunk. I'm going to sleep over at a friend's."

"Where are you? I'll come pick you up."

"No," he insisted. "It's fine. I'll see you tomorrow…"

Then he hung up.

I called back and the phone went straight to voicemail. I tried several times again that night, then several times again the next morning. No answer. Around noon, my phone rang.

"I'm heading home," he informed me.

Now it was my turn to say no. My initial burst of relief that Nathan was okay evaporated in the raging heat of my frustration and disappointment. My fingers clenched the phone so hard they hurt—releasing the phone almost made them cramp later. I fought to keep my voice from shaking. "Don't come home. If you want to be single, you can be single."

"What?" he said. "Okay, whatever." I could imagine him on the other end of the line, cradling his head from a hangover and maybe rolling a joint with his other hand. Maybe he was with company. Maybe it wasn't exactly friendly company. It took every ounce of my willpower not to throw the phone across the room once he hung up on me.

He showed up later on that Sunday afternoon to grab a few things to "go stay at a friend's house."

"You're not staying?" I stared at him for a moment, nearly as dumbfounded as I was angry. "What is this? Do you not want to be married anymore?"

"This is just not working." He didn't look at me as he tossed his toothpaste and toothbrush into a small duffel bag. "It's just not. We tried going to therapy, we tried going to church—nothing helps. I want a break."

"A break?" I repeated. "There are no breaks in marriage. We either work it out or we don't."

He didn't reply.

My heart pattered a million miles a minute, beating like the wings of a butterfly as it tries to escape from the sticky web of a spider, knowing what would happen, trying to tell me something I didn't want to admit. Part of me wanted to beg, to reach out to him, to grab his arms and shake some sense into him and make him fight for us and our future. Part of me wanted to slap him, to shove him away, to scream at him for letting me waste so much time and love on him. My pride won, forcing me to keep my chin up and my voice clipped and cold.

"If you don't want to be married anymore, that's fine with me!"

"Fine," he said.

...

After Nathan left, I cried. I didn't crumple to the floor like my mom had after my dad had left that one time, with all of us kids gathered around her. I stood, instinctively wrapping my arms around my chest and stomach, as if cradling my broken heart and broken wings. I remember crying until I could barely breathe, until I wheezed for air.

No air.

No faith.

I knew this was the end.

Of course, it wasn't *the end*. Sometimes I forgot it, but deep down I knew the truth. Sometimes an end is just the end of a beginning, making way for the next chapter in your life.

30

THE END OF THE BEGINNING

When I could breathe again, I called Natalie, thankful for the silver lining of having a good friend who was a paralegal. That Sunday afternoon she was working at the law firm, putting in extra hours. "I want a divorce," I said. She invited me to meet her at the law firm, where she gave me a big hug and sat me down to talk and ensure that it was really what I wanted.

"I'm sorry this is happening," she consoled me when I explained my reasons, "but it's probably for the best." Natalie could be tough as nails and sweet as honey depending on the circumstance, and that's why I adored her. "Do you have somewhere to stay?"

I didn't. We'd already foreclosed on the loft and had moved into a rental home, which was Nathan's; I couldn't afford moving out on my own. My mother had moved on her own to a one-bedroom apartment and was housing pregnant Laila; they wouldn't have room for me, much less for me and two dogs. Natalie invited me to come stay at her apartment with her and my niece and nephew.

I stayed with Natalie for a few days. Nathan returned home a week or so later; leading up to Valentine's Day, we spent a few numb days together, suffocated by tension and unspoken frustrations. Looking back, I'm not sure why I stuck around a while longer. Perhaps a small part of me hoped that February 14 had enough magic to glue back the broken pieces of our marriage. But Valentine's was just one flimsy day. Nathan was working all night—or said he was—and I spent the evening drinking wine with Natalie at her place. Later that night, I logged onto Facebook and saw a guy named Adam had been messaging me: *I think your man Nathan is cheating on you with my girlfriend.*

I think the day won the award for my worst Valentine's Day to date.

The very next day, my brothers helped me move most of my things out, and I gradually moved in with Natalie; on February 16, I submitted my papers for divorce. Natalie showed up to present Nathan with the divorce papers and get his signature.

"I don't want a divorce," he told her.

Well, too bad for him.

He eventually agreed to it, as I knew he would. After a five-year relationship that included two-and-a-half years of marriage, Nathan and I parted very amicably despite all that had happened; he agreed to pay some alimony to help pay my rent given that I'd been unable to return to any semblance of a steady work schedule due to the nightmarish whirl of miscarriages and seizures. Natalie was a godsend, proving her compassion and her reliability in my time of need. I initially took Jerome with me along with Diamond, but my heart broke when I realized I had to give Jerome—too active, too big, and too hyper to be happy in a cramped apartment filled with four people—back to Nathan.

Worst of all, I realized that when I broke up with Nathan, I broke up with his family as well. I'd never had a dad look out for me and be there for me—without an agenda, without a tendency for violence, and just with love—as Nathan's dad did. Nathan's mom treated me more as a daughter than as a daughter-in-law and actively pursued cultivating a mature and loving relationship with me. Meanwhile, my mom seemed more concerned about getting the things from the house rather than checking on my fractured heart. It killed me that she constantly seemed to give me less and less attention because I had apparently been "doing well" and her other children "needed her" more. Didn't I deserve a mom, too?

Though the divorce was difficult—and time-consuming (given all the paperwork, Nathan's stalling, and administrative nonsense, our divorce was officially filed in June and finalized in August)—it was one of the best decisions I'd ever made in my life. Adam and I met up for drinks a few days after I saw his Facebook messages and we exchanged our sides of the story, piecing together everything that had gone down and confirming each other's suspicions. I found out that Adam had been the boyfriend of a girl with whom Nathan had been cheating while we'd been together.

It hurts like hell when a person you once loved and cared about—and who once loved you back, to whatever degree and for however long—dismisses you and your feelings, totally disrespects you, and thinks that it's okay.

Grow up.

With a shred of decency, a human being doesn't do that to a stranger, much less a partner. One year before this whole mess, I'd raised the red flag and told him our relationship was in trouble and I wasn't happy. He'd gotten on his knees, crying, and had begged me to stay—and look where that had that gotten us! If Nathan wanted to break up, he should have been honest with me as I'd been with him. He could have spoken up and ended things. There'd been no need to play at therapy, to blame it on the weed, to go sneaking behind my back.

Betrayal didn't sting any less—especially because Nathan and I had been together when he'd had his affair (or affairs)—but I felt validated that I'd dumped Nathan before I'd had solid evidence of his infidelity. This was the straw that broke the camel's back; our relationship had died a long time ago, and there was nothing to hold on to any longer. Adam and I toasted to our freedom. The next day, I called my brothers, rented a truck, and had them pack up everything—the bed, the couch, the table, the TV, the blankets, the pots and pans, and so on. I enjoyed the idea of Nathan the Cheater coming home to an empty house.

After breaking up with Nathan, I let the rage and remorse take its course—rage at his infidelity, remorse for the future he'd destroyed and for my blindness. Why had I been so blind, so stupid? Perhaps deep down, I'd known—I'd sensed all of this wrongness—but I just didn't want to face it. As has often been the case in my times of turmoil, I spent a few days holed up in the local library. I came across a little red book that coached readers on how to get over a divorce in thirty days. I borrowed it and treasured it like a little Bible, reading portions of it day by day as it walked me through the stages of grief. When I reached the final step—*take one day to cry until you run out of tears while looking at the wedding photos and then burn them up or tear them to pieces*—I felt ready to move on.

I donated my wedding dress, sold my wedding ring, put some of my furniture in storage and sold the rest, and decided that my chapter with Nathan was a life lesson meant to make me stronger and smarter. When that J. Cole rap song came out years later, I'd sing along and smile. You know the one—about getting fooled thrice. Look it up if you don't know what I'm talking about; it's a good one.

Trust your instincts, dear reader. Don't think you can change people. Don't pressure them to be with you—it will never work out, as I learned the hard way. If they want to become better people, they'll work to improve by themselves. If they want to be with you, they'll stay. If they love you, they'll want to spend time with you and your happiness will become a priority. Love yourself enough to demand being treated like you're enough, because *you are enough*—you are more than enough! Speak your mind and don't give anyone the power to walk all over you. Only you control your life. Your destiny is what you make of it. And when people hurt you, forgive them.

Forgive them and *move on*.

PART 5
2010—2016

"WE DO NOT NEED MAGIC TO CHANGE THE WORLD. WE CARRY ALL THE POWER WE NEED INSIDE OURSELVES ALREADY: WE HAVE THE POWER TO IMAGINE BETTER."

—J. K. ROWLING

31

Kissing Frogs

Nathan's alimony had my rent covered for six months, but I'd need cash for utilities, groceries, car payments, and other necessities. I couldn't sit around waiting for things to change. My family didn't have the means to lend me money and I may have been too proud to take it anyway. Nobody was going to show up and just dump a miracle into my hands.

I secured a job at a local company as an admin coordinator, working on trademarks, finances, and data entry. The commute was an hour, the work was dull, and the position was lower than anything I'd taken on before, but I'd been out of work for a year and it hadn't been easy to find something on such short notice. My manager humiliated me and my colleagues like it was her job—one she enjoyed very much. With her straw-like hair, beady eyes, and constant snarky criticism, she reminded me of a fairy-tale witch. I half-expected to see her appear in front of me each morning with a big mole on her chin and an enchanted apple in her hand.

A job was a job, though, and it helped me gain back my financial independence.

At least I had Natalie, my godsend and my silver lining. I truly believe that God has a way of revealing who the guardian angels in our lives are when we need it most. A month after I moved in, Natalie's lease drew to an end; we decided to take on a year-long joint lease and moved into a three-bedroom apartment together to give us, the kids, and Diamond more breathing space. I spent time with Jasmine too, who was happily married to Logan but still made time for me. As the days and weeks and months passed, I found myself again.

For the first time in my life, I decided to start putting myself first. That meant, above all, taking care of my health. I read as much as I could about epilepsy and decided that I would do whatever I could to never have another seizure again. I began exercising more, trying out a few things until I found something I really enjoyed: turbo kickboxing! I began eating more healthfully, eventually choosing to go vegan. I reached out to my mom and siblings more, reminding myself that relationships are always a two-way street, that love begets love, and that my mother really *did* love me as best as she could in her own way. I began feeling better about myself; I had a job, I could pay my bills, my health was under control, and I loved my housemates.

Still, in the depths of my soul, I felt the loneliness sometimes. Something was missing.

I watched Natalie go out on her dates and she'd invite me along whenever she had the urge to go partying. I joined her sometimes and enjoyed the evenings out, but I didn't really feel motivated to invest my time in getting to know anybody. For a while, Natalie didn't bug me about it, letting me take my time. Then we met up with Seiko one night, and the two of them apparently decided that my time for moping and healing was up.

That's how I started kissing frogs.

...

I walked through the front door of our apartment one evening to find Natalie enjoying a glass of wine on the couch, waiting up for me after she'd put the kids to bed. There was a second glass empty and ready for me on the table.

Natalie looked up as I came in, took one look at my face, and started filling the glass.

"Worse than Butter Teeth?" she asked. Butter Teeth was a guy I'd met at the dimly lit bar who looked great with his closed-lipped smile. In broad daylight, he'd parted his lips and revealed the worst set of yellowed teeth I'd ever seen. Our first date had lasted five minutes before I'd excused myself due to a "friend's emergency." It'd been our last.

"Natalie." I plopped down next to her and unwound my scarf from around my neck. "Any chance I'm aging backward and I'm really just fifteen years old right now?"

"No..." My friend glanced over at me as she refilled her own glass. "As far as I know, there was only one Benjamin Button."

"Then explain why my date bought me a child ticket tonight."

Natalie gasped and giggled. "At the movies? He didn't!"

"Girl, the man was so cheap I think he'd sell his skin if it would save him from buying soap."

"Oh no..."

"So get this. Before the movie begins, he asks me if I want something to drink or eat. I tell him I'd like a soda. Just a soda—no biggie, right? He gets a large and asks for two straws. Like he expects me to share his spit?" I rolled my eyes. "It's the first date—I don't know him! After we go get seated, I just walk back to the concession stand and I buy my own drink. When I get back he says, 'Oh, you should have said you wanted your own.'"

Natalie face-palmed herself. "At least he wasn't competing for a local Oscar."

We both began laughing at that, then laughed even harder once we started shushing each other so we wouldn't wake the kids.

Oscar was the first guy I began dating soon after Natalie started dragging me out of the house to go clubbing with her. Oscar wasn't his real name, of course. He wasn't the cutest or the brightest—he was divorced with kids, had a roommate, and was a struggling "actor" who worked in construction during the day—but we were both lonely and physically attracted to each other. We helped each other stave off the solitude for a month or so until I decided a meaningless relationship was no better than a dead-end marriage. He claimed he was an actor because he'd once appeared on *The People's Court* as an extra. At one point he bragged to me that he'd won a local Oscar. What the hell was a local Oscar? When I'd told Natalie, we'd both laughed until we'd cried.

"Maybe the next guy will be better," Natalie said.

"I don't know." I swirled my wine gently in the cup, careful not to slosh any on the couch. "I mean, remember Business Guy? He was the real deal, wasn't he? Charming, handsome, smart…" Seiko had set me up with Business Guy and it'd been a generous match; though he was in his early fifties and divorced, Business Guy's children were grown and he was a successful business owner. He was gentlemanly, stylish, and handsome.

"You said there was no chemistry," Natalie reminded me. It was true. When Business Guy had kissed me goodnight on our date, there hadn't been a single spark. As much as I willed it, I couldn't feel excited with him.

"Okay." I took a deep breath, set my glass down, and faced Natalie determinedly. "I trust you. You have to tell me the truth. Is there something wrong with me?"

"Nothing's wrong with you." She smiled at me. "You've got to kiss a lot of frogs before you find that prince. But you've changed, you know."

"Changed?" The word caught me by surprise. "I guess I'm older. Pickier. You think I'm turning into an old maid?" I joked.

"At thirty-one? Connie, you and I were the life of the party last weekend. Didn't anybody tell you thirty is the new twenty?"

"I wouldn't want to relive my twenties again," I remarked. "I guess it's good to leave that decade behind me."

"Yes," she said. "You know what I think? You're tougher. Smarter. You've shed old skin and grown new armor. You've proven yourself, you've made something of yourself, and you know it. You've got standards now. I think you know what you want in life."

"Maybe," I conceded with a grateful smile. She didn't need to compliment me, didn't gain anything because of it, yet she did anyway. Sometimes I felt that she believed in me more than I believed in myself, buoying me up like a breeze uplifting a tired butterfly. "I know I don't want Butter Teeth."

Natalie laughed. "Can't blame you. Hey, why don't you try online dating? Widen your network a little bit."

"Um, no." I shook my head and finished the glass of wine. "No weirdos or serial killers for me. Thanks but no thanks."

"Don't be silly. I know people who have tried it with great success. Just think about it as another way to meet people whom you don't have the opportunity to meet otherwise in your current circle." Natalie watched me consider it. "Come on, give it a chance. You don't get out that much. Look, we can both sign up. It gives you a seven-day free membership. What have you got to lose?"

"Okay," I finally agreed. "Seven days. That's it. And if it's full of frogs, I'm out."

. . .

I signed up as *AlluringSweetn*, describing myself as a thirty-one-year-old based in San Diego, interested in males thirty to fifty-two years old. My byline was: *I'm very discreet...but I will haunt your dreams.*

In my online bio, I wrote about my love of San Diego, my obsession with turbo kickboxing, my big travel bucket list, and my guilty pleasures of dark chocolate, popcorn, and romantic walks on the beach. I talked about how I loved reading and watching movies, and about how I liked socializing with my tight circle of friends, enjoyed my own company, and was looking for someone special to spend time with. I described myself as thoughtful, sweet, energetic, happy, and fun, and wanted someone who shared those same qualities.

If you like what you read and see…send me a note or a wink, I concluded.

Notes and winks abounded on a daily basis. I found the whole process pretty overwhelming. There was an enormous response for both of us when we signed up from all sorts of people, but I guess that's what happened whenever online users sniffed out fresh blood. It made me even more apprehensive about this whole online dating thing.

When our seven days were almost up, I decided to buy a month of membership. I'd gotten many messages in seven days and I wanted a chance to weed through that garden before giving up on it altogether. Three weeks into that first month, Natalie questioned me about my progress. "Have you met anyone interesting yet?"

"No."

Natalie raised an eyebrow. She knew me well. "Have you logged on at all since last week?"

"No," I admitted again.

Natalie shook her head. "One week left, girl. Come on, please, at least set up a few dates!"

What have I got to lose? I thought. *Just do it.* I set up five dates for that last week—different sorts of guys, different ethnicities, different age groups—and decided to let the chips fall where they may. I let Natalie's excitement fuel me. Her optimism was contagious. Who knew? Maybe I'd fall too. Maybe in love. Or maybe on my face.

If you never try, you'll never know.

32

MEETING MY MATCH

The main reason I decided to sign up for one month of membership was because I'd received a message from a guy who introduced himself as Mr. Energetic, Happy, and Fun, automatically promising some of the qualities I was looking for. His note was brief and sweet, and I wrote back after I studied his profile and his handsome photo. He described himself as *a down-to-earth guy who enjoys the simple things in life*. He'd *recently found a love for experimenting in the kitchen* and he *does 4K mud runs* for fun during the weekends. He wrote that *nights on the town are low key* and claimed he was *looking for a best friend...*

His name was Claude Jones, and he sounded too good to be true.

After a day or two passed without a response from him, I decided he *had* been too good to be true. The next time I sat down in front of my computer again, however, a pop-up in my inbox notified me that I'd received a new message.

Hello Constance,

Before I responded I wanted to know if you still wanted to chat…I don't have access to your profile so I didn't know if you made it hidden or if your membership expired.

Let me know if you are still interested in keeping in touch.

Claude

I bit my lip but I couldn't stop myself from smiling. My fingers flurried across the keyboard as I shot back a response.

Yes, I am still interested. I have been getting a ton of emails and winks and many of them have been from people that do not have the attributes I am looking for. So I made my profile hidden when I am not online…

I added a few things about attending a party with my roommate over the weekend and celebrating a friend's birthday at a new restaurant downtown.

Claude responded almost immediately.

Constance, I hope you're having a great start to your week. Sounds like your weekend was fun-filled. My weekend was low-key. I hung out with the guys on Saturday, we call ourselves the wolf pack. We try and get together once a month just to catch up and release some stress. On Sunday I went to a beach concert in Encinitas. They have them every other Sunday. It's a good time to chill, enjoy the sun, and people watch.

I think your turbo kickboxing is unique! I can't knock it 'cause it's working for you. I mix up my workout with running and weights. I'm trying to maintain and just stay healthy.

So since you're an adventurer, what sort of places do you want to visit? Are you more of a backpacker or do you enjoy tropical places? On my list, I want to visit New Zealand, Argentina, and Austria. I'd love a Europe trip in general and I also want to try a cruise of some sort.

Sorry about the profile mix-up; when you originally replied to my email, I checked your profile and it said you were not visible...

Well, have a great day. Talk with you soon.

Claude

Throughout the week, whenever Claude messaged me, I didn't—or couldn't—respond quickly. He passed along his personal email and his cell number. Life and work kept me preoccupied, a friend was visiting from out of town, I was stuck in traffic, or there was no "good time" to sit down and breathe and compose a perfect message to my charming pen-pal. He persisted though, making me a part of his day, telling me about his work schedule as a computer engineer at Yahoo! and his outings with his friends, sending me pictures of his mud run experience and inviting me to the next such run in October.

That Friday evening, I reread the closing paragraph of his latest email.

Regarding plans for the weekend...if you are not busy on Sunday and are open to meeting, I would like to plan something with you. When you have time this evening, give me a call and we can chat... and if you feel like hanging out on Sunday we can talk about trying to make it happen...I have a few ideas.

Talk to you soon and enjoy the rest of your day.

I took a deep breath and reached for my cell phone.

33

A New Beginning

Three days and a few emails after his first message, I met up with Claude on a Sunday at 2 p.m. We met for lunch at Roppongi's, a quaint little tapas and sushi bar restaurant in La Jolla. It was hot and sunny, a perfect July day in 2011. I wore my favorite sundress and felt my heart pattering excitedly despite the little voice in my head warning me that this could just be one more big mistake. I hid my high hopes behind my sunglasses.

A man walked over toward the restaurant—tall, dark, handsome, and totally oblivious to the fact that I was spying on him. I watched him from my car, parked nearby. I'd arrived early to get a peek of what he looked like and how he behaved, just to make sure that I really did feel okay with going through with the date. He walked up to the front entrance of the restaurant and stood outside, looking around as if scanning the street to spot me. His face looked relaxed and kind, though his eyes were hidden by sunglasses. He seemed to hold himself with confidence and poise. When a family walked up toward the door of the restaurant, pushing a baby carriage and trying to keep their two other kids in hand, Claude immediately reached over and opened the restaurant door for them with a smile. They smiled back and thanked him.

My trepidation evaporated. I shot him a text: I see you. Then I got out of the car and walked over to the restaurant.

"Constance?" he said as I approached. He looked just like Claude—Claude wearing sunglasses, that is.

"Claude." I smiled. "Hi."

"It's great to meet you."

"Good to meet you too."

We gave each other a tentative, one-armed hug, his warmness and positivity rolling in almost tangible ripples from his body to mine as he wrapped an arm around my shoulders. It made me smile wider.

"Should we sit?"

"Yes, this is a pretty place."

"You haven't been here before?"

I shook my head no.

"I like it; I come here to eat sometimes. The food is really good. I like to sit and read or just people-watch."

"That's awesome." We navigated around the tables and I paused at one I liked; he immediately raised an eyebrow and half-gestured at the table. I nodded and smiled, feeling amused—it was like we'd been together so many years that we could decide where to sit just by looking at each other. "Some people don't like to eat alone. I like it sometimes."

"Me too."

We sat down across from each other. A mutual question hung between us like a fruit of Eden, ripe for the taking: *Who are you? Who are you, really?*

"You look even better in person," Claude said. "You're beautiful."

"Thank you. I can't see you fully, though. Do you mind taking off your sunglasses? I want to see your eyes."

He chuckled and immediately removed them. "Like what you see?"

"You have long lashes!" I laughed. "I'm jealous." I *did* like what I saw. His smile was nice. His eyes were warm and golden-brown like sun-kissed honey. He looked at me and began chipping away at the thorns I'd built around the garden of my heart.

A waiter showed up and handed us our menus. We studied our choices, then ordered our drinks: a rum neat for Claude and a cucumber martini for me. "By the way," I told him, "just so you don't think I'll be bailing on you later, I want to let you know that I've got to attend my brother's birthday barbecue in a couple of hours."

"No problem," Claude said, but I could also tell that he understood the underlying message. *Okay,* his smiling eyes told me. *I get that you're nervous and I accept your need for a get-out strategy in case this goes badly. But I promise it won't…I'll do my best to make sure we enjoy this…*

For a moment, I found myself thinking that I didn't want drinks and tapas anymore. I wanted a crystal ball. I wanted someone to grab my shoulder and say, *Hey, it's okay. He's a good one. Go for it. Fall for him. Enjoy it. I've seen the future; it's golden.* I wanted to see the trailer of the rest of my life and see if it held more dread and fear and heartache. I didn't want to fall in love with a guy just to get hurt all over again. How many times could a heart be broken? How many times could trust be trampled? How many years could a butterfly fight to emerge from its cocoon?

It could end badly, I told myself, agreeing with the voice of fear screaming in my head. *It could hurt. But I'm stronger now. I'm smarter. I'll get out fast. I'll get out first.*

Or…it might be beautiful. It might be different. It might be more real than anything else. Stars can't shine without the darkness. Maybe it's not him, maybe it's somebody else, but God has plans…and I've got better judgment now.

The voice in my head quieted. I felt ready. I wanted to give Claude a chance. I'd never hear the end of it if I told Natalie I bailed on him just because I was nervous.

"So what made you decide to try Match?" Claude asked, breaking through my thoughts.

"A friend thought I should try it." I shrugged to show that it wasn't a big deal, but I found myself blushing. "She bugged me about it for a few weeks so I gave it a shot."

"Have you been on any other Match dates?" The way he looked at me was intoxicating. With every question, Claude leaned in toward me a little bit more, minimizing the distance between us, bringing our hearts physically closer. Without realizing it at first, I found myself gradually leaning in toward him too. It was almost as if he was magnetic.

"Not yet," I admitted. "You're my first. What about you? Have you been on Match long? How many dates have you been on?"

"I've been on about three months. And yeah, I've been on a few dates, but obviously I haven't found anyone I like or with whom I really had a connection with. But I liked talking with you." He grinned at me. "So, tell me about you. I know you're from San Diego…where did you go to school?"

One question led to another. I found myself opening up to Claude just as he opened up to me. We laid all our cards on the table, both of us opting to be as straightforward as possible. I found out he'd gotten married when he was twenty-one and had divorced after ten years; we spoke a bit about why we'd both left our respective first marriages behind. His partner had cheated on him, too. We'd both been pained by those experiences, but we'd sensed that letting go had been for the best.

"Do you still believe in marriage?" Whether or not things would progress between us was beside the point; in that moment, I was genuinely curious. What was the perspective of someone else who had walked in my shoes? "Would you get married again?"

"Yes, I do. I could see myself getting married again. You?"

"I don't know. I've read that second marriages have a higher rate of divorce, and I don't want to end up with a second divorce."

"Then don't." Claude smiled at me until I smiled back, lightening the mood. "Make sure it's right the next time."

About halfway through the date, I excused myself to go to the restroom. I felt Claude's eyes on me as I walked away, and I couldn't help swaying my hips a bit more than usual, feeling giddy and light. Once I had the privacy of the restroom to myself, I quickly dialed Natalie's number, skimming through her number of texts.

"So?" she urged. "How is it going?"

"It's going great. Everything's fine. He seems nice!"

"Good!" Natalie said. "You weren't responding to any of my texts! I wanted to make sure he hadn't kidnapped you."

By the time I walked back to the table, I'd decided that I didn't have to attend the birthday barbeque that day—it was more of a gathering for friends, since my family already had celebrated my brother with a smaller party the night before—and told Claude so. He suggested extending the date by getting some coffee and heading over to the movie theater to see if anything interesting was playing. We ended up seeing *Friends with Benefits,* which was rather ironic but still a great movie and fun love story.

When Claude walked me to my car that night after spending over eight hours with me, I felt as if time had sped by much faster than usual. Right before we parted ways, he drew me into his arms and kissed me—carefully first, then more passionately once I began kissing him back. The butterflies in my stomach erupted in flight, fluttering in every direction. I felt my face get warm and my body tingled. I melted against him, savoring him, delighted by the delicious headiness of his lips and the protective tenderness of his embrace.

I knew, deep in my heart, that I'd be seeing a lot more of Claude Jones. That night, when I got home, Natalie was waiting up for me. She practically pounced when I walked through the door.

"So…?" she asked.

"Oh my God, Natalie…"

She giggled at my excitement. "Yeees…?"

I took a deep breath. "I think I'm in love."

34

CJ + CJ

Claude and I started seeing each other regularly, getting to know one another, finding out what foods we enjoyed and our favorite movies, where we wanted to travel and what bad dates we'd suffered through. We talked about his obsession with running and weight-lifting as a way of clearing his head and getting in shape; we talked about my passion with turbo kickboxing and how much fun I had with it. Claude promised he'd get me to like running and I laughed in his face. Who would have guessed that two years later, I'd be competing in a mud run right along with him!

Always having my back, Natalie, Jasmine, and Logan had interrogated him shortly after we started dating. They approved. Claude was for real. He *is* for real. He was all he said he was—and more. He loved experimenting in the kitchen, setting up Pandora and breaking out the pots and pans and letting inspiration overtake him. He enjoyed his active lifestyle and his low-key evenings; he was as happy reading a book as he was watching a movie. He knew the little things in life—a nice dinner, a fine glass of wine, a stimulating conversation, a tender kiss—are actually the big things, the important things. He was tough and smart, a software engineer who was also passionate about coaching others to reach their full potential. He was smart and he was sexy and he was kind.

Claude always had a smile ready for me, but the world hadn't always smiled back at him. For many years, he'd been haunted by an abusive home and a traumatic childhood. He would go to school with bruises on his body from his stepfather's beatings—bruises only in areas where the clothes covered his skin so that nobody else would see the truth. His stepfather beat, insulted, stole money from, and ridiculed him regularly, constantly calling him stupid no matter how many times Claude tried to prove him wrong by bringing home straight A's. Claude grew up too fast, forced to take care of his three younger brothers while his military parents traveled. He never met his biological father. Claude had a quiet yet fiery spirit and an entrepreneurial attitude; he sold candy in high school and saved up enough money to get his heart's desire: a Super Nintendo.

Claude fell in love with me, unafraid to take another chance at life. Realizing our similarities in our pasts yet also in our current perspectives on life, we also realized that we were at a point in our lives where not only did we *know* what we truly wanted—we knew better than to take it for granted. We unfolded and exposed our tightly clenched hearts as if they were roses that unfurled one petal at a time. He called me his butterfly, unaware that he was a butterfly, too. Life had molded him, giving him enough pain and uncertainty to ensure that he built thick armor. His heart had guided him, giving him the tenacity and trust to emerge from his cocoon better rather than bitter, a man who was brilliantly and beautifully made.

By November, we'd moved in together. Four months to the day we'd met, Claude invited me out to lunch one day. We extended the date and hung out at a cozy Starbucks nearby, reading a couple's compatibility book of questions. Between my coffee and his hot cocoa, we were impressed to see that we matched up on every single one of the questions we asked each other. I don't think it shocked us, though. Sometimes you just *know*, but it doesn't hurt when emotion is reinforced with logic. That crisp November evening we went home together and spent some time curled up on the couch, watching a TV show.

Suddenly, Claude slipped away to "run upstairs a sec." I waited as the seconds passed. After about fifteen minutes, I went upstairs to check on him.

I tried the master bedroom first, thinking that it was strange for the door to be closed; when I tried turning the knob, it was locked. I knocked. Claude didn't answer. I frowned and went back downstairs. *Maybe he's in the bathroom,* I reassured myself. *He would have called out to me if something was wrong.*

Sure enough, Claude appeared downstairs a few minutes later. "I had to use the bathroom," he explained apologetically. Then he handed me a card. "Oh, and this is for you."

Suspicious, I held the envelope in my hand and gently squeezed the bottom, half-expecting to feel a ring within it. I didn't. I opened the envelope, read the card, and kissed him. *You are my world,* he'd written, *my one and only. I never knew I could find happiness like this... Take care of my heart and I will take care of yours. We're in it to win it, baby! CJ + CJ forever...*

Claude was expressive; he'd confessed his feelings for me verbally, in emails, and in this card, but he also expressed his love in actions. He'd helped me when my car had broken down and hunted for a new one. He'd accepted me for all my flaws and imperfections; my past, my epilepsy, and my emotional, physical, and mental battle scars did not matter to him. And I found it incredible that he could electrify me, body and soul, with just a kiss.

"In it to win it," I promised back. It had become our mantra, our motto, our daily vow. "I love you too..."

He took my hand and led me upstairs. When he opened the door to the master bedroom, I found myself facing a little paradise of cozy candles, with flower petals and dark chocolate candy forming heart shapes on the bed. I gasped and turned around.

Claude got down on one knee. I gasped again. Even though part of me had gotten enough hints to know what was coming, it still felt unreal, unbelievable, and too good to be true. He took a little black box out of his pocket and asked me to marry him.

I wept this time. From all his hints about wanting to spend the rest of our lives together, I wasn't completely shocked at the proposal, but I was shocked by the ocean of emotions I felt. I was excited, elated, hopeful, and so indescribably happy.

Of course I said yes. When he placed the ring on my finger, it was as if he placed his heart—as fragile as a butterfly, as beautiful as a tiny world—in my hands and asked me: *Please don't crush it. Here, take it. Here, I'm yours.*

There was lots of hugging and kissing. "I didn't know if I'd ever find my match," he said when he managed to get a word in edgewise. "But I have. I want to spend the rest of my life with you, Constance Grays."

"Well, soon-to-be Constance Jones," I corrected him through my tears, and he kissed me again.

I'd fallen in love with him and I felt loved in return. He knew me and accepted me. When he called me his friend, his lover, and his partner-in-crime, I believed him. Nobody had compelled him to desire me or marry me. This was it. He loved me. I loved him.

I'd met my match at last.

35

INTO THE WOODS

Two weeks after Claude and I got engaged, I lost my job at the startup I'd been working at. I didn't particularly miss the environment or my witchy supervisor—and it was only a matter of time anyway since the company was downsizing—but getting let go hurts no matter the cause. I'll never forget my drive home that day. My hands shook and I had to pull over twice because I was crying too hard to focus on the road. I had flashbacks to the last time I'd lost my job, back when I'd been with Nathan; that had been nothing short of devastating. The worst thing was that I'd just moved in with Claude and I hated to think that *he* would think I was using him.

I broke the news to Claude, unable to stop the tears from sliding down my cheeks. I hated the feeling of being dependent. Stripped of my sense of independence and worth, I felt naked and needy. Claude calmed me down and told me that my situation was an opportunity in disguise.

"I know you hated that job," he said, also knowing that I'd refused to quit unless I first found something else to serve as my source of income. He held me in his arms and tucked some loose hair behind my ear. "Sweetie, what do *you* really want to do in your life?"

Nobody had ever really asked me that before.

I qualified for unemployment, which gave me enough of a breather to consider what I really wanted. I'd read that a person's true calling lies in where their passion and society's needs intersect. I loved baking and I loved dogs; I did some research and found there was a market for gourmet dog treats. "This is what I want," I told Claude a couple of days later, showing him some photos online.

"Okay," he replied. "If that's what you want, I support you. We're in this together—we're in it to win it. Let's see how it's done."

It turned out to be much more complicated than I'd initially thought. Once I'd been certified in food handling, gotten a business license, and had designed a logo and website, I found out that a new law came out requiring that I needed to use a commercial kitchen. I found a vendor who could make the treats for me and sell them wholesale, but then there were issues of packaging and delivery and so on…as the requirements added up, I decided this was no longer a low-income startup idea. Without an initial source of income, I simply didn't have the resources to continue.

When I chucked the idea and began job hunting again, Claude told me about his job at Walmart Labs, where he worked as a senior director in the software engineering department. He'd started a remote office with a small group of staff; a year in, they'd moved to a larger space and needed a site manager. Back then, knowing I wasn't keen about my job, Claude had asked me if I was interested. Initially, I had turned down the offer. Now, three months later, the person they'd hired had left the position and I'd just been laid off. Claude asked me again.

"Not interested," I reassured him. "I don't think it's a good idea for us to work together." I'd heard that couples who work together tend to bring work issues home. Worse, couples who work together sometimes got bored of each other after being together twenty-four/seven.

"You'd be in a different department with a different manager," he assured me. "I think you're a good candidate. Why not try? If this doesn't work out, we'll try something else. But what have you got to lose?"

Claude offered logical arguments. I reconsidered and sent in my resume. I reported into a different department, content that Claude had nothing to do with the interview process. I was interviewed five times by different people before I received the job offer. My heart swelled when I called Claude to tell him the news.

"I knew you could do it," he said. "I'm so proud of you!"

I could hear him smiling through the phone. I felt myself grinning like a maniac. *We really are in it to win it,* I thought. Best of all, we were out of the woods. God had tested our commitment to each other, and we'd proven ourselves. Claude had believed in me and supported me. I'd gotten back on my feet and had secured my independence with a new job.

How little I still knew!

We weren't out of the woods.

We hadn't even walked into them yet.

...

Things were certainly looking up. Claude and I were settled and happy, hard-working and healthy. At Walmart Global eCommerce, I proudly worked as a site manager among an amazing crew of software engineers, data scientists, designers, and product managers. I flexed my creativity and team-bonding skills to create a culture of acceptance, inclusion, and diversity. At work and at home, I had found a sanctuary: a place where people's values aligned with mine, where I could build dreams, where I could find purpose and chase self-improvement one day at a time.

In the autumn of 2013, over a year and a half into our relationship, a little miracle happened. Claude and I had attended a friend's wedding, where we'd had a wonderful time. We'd gone home—drunk in love and perhaps a bit tipsy—to have an even more wonderful time, and we might have been reckless. Later that month, my period was late.

When I purchased a pregnancy test and locked myself in the bathroom, I told myself that it was just a routine check and just to calm myself down. I sat on the toilet and waited a couple of minutes, watching as two telltale red lines appeared on the pregnancy stick. My breathing quickened. Thanks to the fertility I'd apparently inherited from my mother and the epilepsy medication that nulled whatever birth control pills I tried, here I was again: pregnant.

Uh-oh, I thought. *How do I tell Claude?*

I decided it was best to get it over with. I texted him a picture of the pregnancy test.

He immediately texted me back: What is that?

You know what it is, I wrote. I didn't write what I was *really* thinking: *Oh my God. What have we done?*

Claude called me, amazed and dazed, and we discussed it in detail that night. We went from *What do we do?* to *Do we want to keep it?* to *Are we ready?* to *Are we selfish even by questioning if we want it keep it?* to *What would our baby look like?*

By dawn, we'd decided that we would become parents. As the days ticked on by, we became more and more okay about the prospect. As the weeks slipped by, we realized we were actually very excited.

I'd been down this road before. I knew better than to have great expectations. Great expectations had almost killed me in the past; they'd stripped me of my health and happiness, they'd helped dismantle a marriage, and they'd sucked me into a black hole of depression. I needed to keep my feet on the ground. By the time we went to the doctor, I was nearly eight weeks pregnant. Our hearts melted when we saw the heartbeat at the hospital. I bombarded the doctors with questions, terrified that the epilepsy meds I took might cause birth defects. I was also worried because I hadn't been taking prenatal vitamins or folic acid. We hadn't planned this pregnancy.

The doctors reassured us that I was okay, telling me we should just keep a close watch on my development. I began to relax. Things would be different this time. I was with Claude, healthy and happy; we were engaged and we were very much in love. Seeing the baby's heartbeat made my pregnancy a reality; torn between apprehension and delight, I called my mother and Natalie and told them the news. In some matters, my apprehension won; I did not tell the rest of my family. Sometimes my delight won; every day, I fell further and further in love with our child.

The regular ultrasound at the twelve-week mark reassured us that there was nothing to worry about. Claude and I bought a home heartbeat monitor and would listen to the baby's heartbeat at night after we curled up in bed together. Some nights we watched videos on baby development or pregnancy movies on Netflix and YouTube. Some nights we just dreamed out loud, brainstorming boy and girl names. I would lie in Claude's arms and snuggle against him in our nest of blankets, realizing that this was my home and heaven: this loving man, this soft bed, this beautiful miracle growing inside me one day at a time.

After twelve weeks, I began to show. For the first time in my life, I witnessed my body changing during pregnancy. My breasts were getting fuller. I was still very slim, but I finally had a little belly bump forming. It was little enough that I could still cover myself with clothes—especially at work—and nobody would be able to tell that I was pregnant. When I was alone at home or by myself at work, I'd run my palms lightly over my ever-so-slightly bulging belly, feeling an indescribable fusion of bliss and wonder. One time I even felt a flutter. My baby was kicking!

We were actually going to have a baby!

...

The weeks slipped by…fourteen, fifteen, sixteen, seventeen, eighteen… Eleven months after our engagement, Claude and I decided to get married. We became official at the local courthouse one crisp and sunny mid-October morning in 2013. It was a quick, traditional, and private ceremony with just one very cherished friend, Jasmine, as our witness. This was a second marriage for both of us; we'd had enough of fanfare and big parties. Originally, it was just going to be Claude and me, but Jasmine wouldn't hear of missing our ceremony; my beautiful Filipino friend arrived earlier than us just to make sure she wouldn't miss it. (*You can't get married without me!* she'd told me. *It's okay, it's just going to be Claude and me,* I'd replied. To which she'd said: *Of course I will be there!*)

Claude and I were declared man and wife, went off to work, and later that day enjoyed a nice dinner together. It was purposefully a private affair, personal and special. Claude and I had both had the big wedding experience before; this time we decided it should be different. We planned to really live it up during our destination wedding and had already scheduled time off from work in January.

Once we reached the nineteenth week of the pregnancy, it was time for the high-risk ultrasound test. We headed to the hospital that morning one hour after I'd drunk the obligatory gallon of water. By the time we were called into the ultrasound room, I had to pee so badly. I undressed, put on the paper gown, and lay down on the examination bed. Claude sat next to me, giving my hand a reassuring squeeze. The ultrasound technician entered the room, greeting us cheerfully.

"I'm going to put some gel on you now," she told me, turning on the machine and giving me a friendly smile. "Normally it's quite cool, but this is a fancy place and we keep it warm."

"Nice," I replied, appreciating both her humor and her thoughtfulness.

She turned to the computer screen, running the probe across my belly with one hand as she studied the results. "Ah yes," she murmured quietly. "There's the feet…see the little legs…do you want to know the gender?"

Claude and I looked at each other, our eyes shining. "Yes!" we said.

"It's a girl," the woman said with a smile.

I let out a mew of joy as Claude squeezed my hand again. *So now we know that we should focus on girl names,* I thought excitedly. *We have to pick the perfect one. A beautiful name for our beautiful little princess!*

The ultrasound technician's hand slowed. She stopped speaking to us. The atmosphere in the room suddenly became heavier. She turned off the machine. "Hold tight," she said. "The doctor will be in, it'll just be a couple minutes."

And she walked out.

FOOTPRINTS IN THE HEART

I didn't like it. The nurse's voice had changed before she left the room. Her eyes, when they met mine, did not reflect her polite smile anymore. My heart began to pound and my eyes sought Claude's.

Please, God, I prayed. *Please let the baby be okay. Not again…not again…not again…*

"Constance, don't you worry." Claude must have seen the terror in my eyes. He kept his voice quiet and soothing. He held my hand and leaned over to kiss my cheek. "The doctor is on his way. We'll see what he'll tell us. It'll be okay."

It felt like years later when the doctor finally appeared, a pale man in his late fifties with a kind face and graying blond hair. He walked in and introduced himself. We greeted him and I felt my smile wobble.

"Let's take a look," he said. He sat down next to me and scanned my belly for a few long moments without saying anything. "Can I do an amnio just to check the fluid and see what's happening with the baby?" he asked at last. He explained that the test put me at a small risk for having a miscarriage, but it was most important to examine the fetus. I nodded and we went through with it. "Okay," he finally said before he exited the room. "Go ahead and get dressed; when you're ready, let's meet in my office."

I peeled the paper gown off slowly, feeling a bit lightheaded. It was as if I was unwrapping layers of my heart—a heart I'd tried to patch back up and take good care of—and was exposing it to the world, leaving it vulnerable and helpless and ready for another beating. *Please, God,* I prayed. Claude helped me pull my dress back on over my head. I slipped on my shoes. We didn't say anything, but I could see his face clouding with worry. He held my hand as we walked to the doctor's office.

Please, God, please…

We entered the room to find the doctor seated behind his desk, rubbing his eyes tiredly. He put on his glasses again when he saw us, and they only seemed to magnify his somber expression. "Have a seat." Once we were seated, he added gently, "I'm sorry to tell you this."

My heart skipped a beat. That's why we were sitting down. No good news ever begins with *I'm sorry to tell you this.*

"Your baby has a condition called congenital hydrocephalus. Constance, Claude, have you ever heard of this condition before? No? Okay, let me explain. In hydrocephalus, the build-up of CSF—the body fluid found in the brain—can raise the pressure inside the skull, which squashes the surrounding brain tissues. In some cases, this can cause the head to steadily grow in size or it can cause convulsions or it may even cause brain damage. Hydrocephalus may be fatal if left untreated. Right now, your baby's head is much larger than the normal range. If you move forward with this pregnancy, your baby could have the following symptoms"—he pushed a sheet of paper toward us from across the desk, a list of symptoms that ranged from sad to terrifying—"and these may last her entire life. It wouldn't be a good quality of life, neither for you nor for her. For example, there would be constant doctor visits to drain the fluid…"

The doctor kept speaking but I could no longer concentrate. I had too much going on. Half of me was battling to listen. The other half of me was battling to keep back a screaming sob that was clawing at my throat to escape.

Claude's voice broke through the haze of my horror. "How did it happen?" he asked the doctor. "Why?"

"I don't know," the doctor said. "The amnio test will tell us more, but it's not as rare as you may think. One in five hundred fetuses have this condition. You are not alone." He explained something else, and then I heard him say, "You are free to get a second opinion, but I truly think you should consider ending the pregnancy."

Consider ending the pregnancy…

The words haunted me all the way out. I don't know how I got up or how I walked out of the office or if I said goodbye to the doctor. I ran into another private hospital room and whirled around to find Claude still with me, tears flooding his eyes.

I have to kill my daughter. I have to end a life. I never even got to meet her.

I opened by mouth and screamed. I couldn't stop the screaming, the tears, the anger, the pain, and the terrible, terrible despair.

I have to kill my daughter. I saw her heart beating. I know she is alive.

Someone or something had found my exposed heart. They were beating at it now, kicking and pummeling and thrashing it until it bled and broke. They killed a little part of my soul.

We need to end this. I have to kill my daughter.

I'd seen movies where mothers had lost their children and they acted as if someone was killing *them*. I'd sympathized—we all do—but I hadn't understood the extent and depth of that pain. I finally understood it now. It hurt to breathe, it hurt to live.

It's a pain I couldn't wish on my worst enemy.

...

Claude and I decided to go through with the abortion.

It was very difficult to find a doctor who would perform a late-term medical abortion on me. It's illegal in most cases. We had to go through so many hoops just to sign up for a doctor who would help us. Between consultations and paperwork, I had to wait almost two weeks for the procedure. Despite her own health issues, my mother came over the weekend before the procedure to stay with us and help me. That Saturday morning as she was resting and reading her Bible in bed, I came into her room and sat down next to her. She rubbed my belly and talked to her granddaughter, telling her how much she loved her and that they would meet in Heaven.

The doctor was right; we weren't alone. Claude and I had our families in this difficult time. Most of all, we had each other. I was glad that we'd held back and hadn't told more than a handful of people about the pregnancy. My siblings found out once it was all over, and some of our friends don't know to this day.

The abortion began with the insertion of laminaria rods, sterile sea-weed sticks—the size of matchsticks—that swell in the cervix and dilate the cervix overnight, ensuring that the abortion process is more safe and effective the next day. The insertion of each such rod was the greatest physical pain I've experienced yet. When it was done, it didn't feel as bad; feeling fine, I went with a friend to have lunch at Panera Bread.

Within a few minutes of being seated, the pain began. I started cramping so bad, I couldn't sit up straight. My friend called Claude and helped me stretch out on the table in our Panera Bread booth. I couldn't sleep all night due to the pain, finally checking into the hospital at 6 a.m., where I had my blood drawn before I was given an anesthetic. Terror engulfed me, my heartache growing along with the physical pain as I knew that each grueling moment brought my daughter's death closer. A tech approached me and inserted the IV. They took me to a room where I undressed, put on the paper gown, and got into the hospital bed. I clung to Claude's hand, heart racing, tears overflowing. The medication kicked in and knocked me out.

When I woke up crying in the recovery room, Claude appeared by my side.

"It's done," he said. "You're okay."

...

I couldn't fathom what had just happened. Mere hours ago, there had been a living being inside of me. I'd heard her heartbeat. I'd seen her on the ultrasound. I'd even felt her kick as she shuffled within my womb.

I'd fantasized about her beautiful bright eyes, her smile, her chortle, the way she'd feel in my arms when I first held her, the incredible and sacred mission of raising her. The notion of having a child after trying so hard was both nerve-wracking and absolutely exhilarating. Every time I traced my hands across my belly, an indescribable wave of compassion, delight, and longing had flooded through my body, warming me with the certainty that I'd do everything in my power to ensure a good life for her.

And now?

Now there was emptiness. Abysmal loss. Anger. Maddening sadness. Despair.

I caressed my belly as if my hands could magically conjure her back inside, back to life, back to how we were paired up so perfectly for the past nineteen weeks.

In that hospital, I was one more statistic. Ten to twenty-five percent of all clinically recognized pregnancies end in miscarriage; I was part of the unlucky 1 percent that suffer through three or more consecutive first-trimester miscarriages. With three prior miscarriages under my belt, my risk for another miscarriage—supposing I could even get pregnant again—was at 43 percent. The statistics meant nothing to me that night.

"Can I see her?" I kept asking. "I want to see her."

The hospital staff told me that it wasn't a good idea because of the type of procedure. They did bring me a consolation card, decorated with her little footprint on it and a quote about how our loved ones leave footprints in our hearts. Right when I had thought I had cried myself dry, I found myself weeping another river. I clutched the pillow to my face to muffle my moans.

The doctors decided I had to stay overnight. Claude went home for a while to care for our pets; the staff did their best to comfort me. At some point I stirred from the bed to visit the restroom. Once I got there, the room faded as I blacked out. When I woke up, the world was sideways. I slowly processed the coldness of the tiles beneath my cheek and the uncomfortable positioning of my limbs. Insult upon injury; it was just what I needed. Luckily a nurse walked in on me and gently helped me back to bed, where she noted that I was anemic because I'd lost a lot of blood during the procedure. A doctor brought me pills to up my iron intake.

Why is this happening? What did I do to deserve this? How can I possibly cope?

The grief of losing a child—no matter the age, no matter the cause—cannot be contained in words. When an unborn child dies within you—usually without even a defined reason—a piece of you seems to die with them. What you face, in the wake of their absence, is unique to you. There is no "right" or "rational" way to cope with a miscarriage, and nobody deserves to tell you otherwise. The loss is physical and emotional, and it can scar you for a long time. The shock strikes like an electric volt. A miscarriage jars you from delight to devastation in no time. The sense of emptiness and helplessness consumes you.

I hated God for punishing me. I hated my body for betraying me. Hadn't I been through enough? At last I begged a nurse for a sedative, complaining about the pain. I let her think that I was referring to the physical pain, but it was my heart that ached the most.

I sobbed myself to sleep, feeling desperately alone. I sensed that this was an emptiness that couldn't be filled or fixed, even by Claude's embrace. Claude and I knew our daughter couldn't have lived a happy or normal life. From all that we had learned from the doctors, we realized her existence would have been riddled with extreme pain and misery, and an inevitable premature death. We believed and believe it was the right thing to do. But writing about this now still gets me teary-eyed.

Getting that abortion was the hardest thing I've done in my life.

37

I Am My Mother's Daughter

That night at the hospital was lifechanging in more ways than one. Having come so close to motherhood myself—the closest I'd ever been—I could finally look upon my mother with a different set of eyes. I felt more empathetic, more comprehending. I realized that we were alike in many ways. I realized that she had often made very difficult decisions for the sake of her family, whether we appreciated it or not. She could have left us at any time. She never did. She could have stopped working to support us throughout her life. She never did. She could have withdrawn from her faith, rejected God, and rejected her instincts to forgive and nurture the people around her despite her own wounds and history. She never did.

I often felt lonely in my big family, like a lamb bleating in the middle of a flock because it has been separated from its mother. There was never enough attention to go around. There were always necessities to attend to: food, clothing, a roof overhead. It was crowded and chaotic at home. For all I know, Evonne was Mother Goose's muse for that famous nursery rhyme—she was the old woman who lived in a shoe, with so many children she didn't know what to do.

My relationship with my mother had always been complicated, perhaps due to the sharp contrast of our lives. She got pregnant in high school, skipped out on college, and raised nine kids without a substantial partner. I was the first in my family to attend and graduate from college, found a man I could rely on, and couldn't have kids. Evonne watched her mother and became exactly like her in many ways; I watched Evonne and learned how I didn't want to live my life.

My mother once told me that I "came into this world grown." That my "independence was something to see." I always acted like "a little woman." That's probably why my sassy grandma liked me so much; most of the time, I didn't act like a little kid. I didn't have the time. It wasn't my luxury. I was far from perfect, though.

And sometimes I exploded.

On my twelfth birthday, I fell asleep dreaming of butterflies—hundreds or thousands of them—that found me in Balboa Park and surrounded me. They placed their little legs on me and tugged at my clothes until I was levitating. Buoyed up by those countless butterflies, I flew through the park and across the world. Then I woke up in the two-bedroom apartment that I shared with all my siblings, excited. Twelve was a magical number. Twelve would be the best year ever!

I was smart enough to know I wouldn't be getting a grand birthday party or an expensive gift. My expectations were realistic. All I wanted for my birthday was a sprinkle cake made by my mom, for me, with love. Instead, my mom—being very busy that day—let my little sisters make the cake while she supervised. In retrospect, it was very sweet that my sisters wanted to make that cake for me, and my mother was trying her best. At the time, however, it felt like a manifestation of her neglect and apathy.

It made me *furious*.

The cake looked great, but I was unhappy. After dinner, my family gathered around and sang *happy birthday*. I blew out the candles and my mom cut the cake. Once I saw that it was plain vanilla—with no birthday sprinkles inside—something in me snapped. I wasn't going to eat that cake and no one else could either! My mom didn't care enough, didn't pay attention enough, didn't love me enough to make me my favorite cake by herself! I smushed the cake with both my hands, destroying the whole thing, and ran away. I slammed the door of the bedroom I shared with all my sisters and sobbed.

As a teenager and young adult, my relationship with my mother continued to be strained. I viewed her as weak and gullible, unable to understand how she could repeatedly forgive and accept my father. I resented her perpetual state of pregnancy, how she welcomed more kids into the world when we could barely make ends meet as we were. I was embarrassed to introduce her to my friends and teachers; my mother sensed this as I grew older, and this may have distanced her in turn. I disagreed with her decision to accept Mia back into our household after she'd been released from jail for stabbing her friend, and with her decision to keep Cricket around for so long despite his bad behavior.

Moving out of the house and attending PLNU helped me find myself and smoothed my relationship with my mother for a time. My first marriage brought us closer; she had meanwhile opened a daycare and was doing better on her own without my dad. Tensions and past hurts continued to resurface. When I was going through my divorce with Adam, I'd given her a lot of my furniture. She asked for more. I had a bike I'd left at Adam's house; when she asked me, "What are you gonna do with that bike?" I was livid.

"Is that all you care about?" I yelled at her. "What you can get?"

My mother had just switched into survival mode, conditioned from years of poverty and need. I took it personally, feeling more alone and abandoned than ever before. I'd felt invisible for most of my childhood—I *hated* the feeling as an adult. Little things snowballed, and I didn't speak to her for months. She wrote me letters asking for my forgiveness, asking for another chance.

My fear of getting hurt again often drove a wedge between us. I missed her even when I pushed her away. I needed a mom. She always seemed to spend time more lavishly on my other siblings, sometimes telling me, "You're doing all right," as if I had no need for her. One year, we agreed to spend Mother's Day together. She had no idea how fiercely I looked forward to it. Instead of hanging out with me, she canceled last minute to go to brunch with my aunt and uncle and their kids. It broke my heart. I cut her off again.

Little things become big things when there's enough history to make them symbolic.

...

Whether he realized it or not, Claude helped us get close again. I guess it makes sense. Love begets love.

It began when, a month into our relationship, Claude mentioned that he was ready to meet my family.

I was not.

If you look up the phrase "family drama," I'm pretty sure you'll find a sketch of my family tree. Could you blame me for wanting to keep Claude to myself for as long as possible? He was so polished, so put-together, so purposeful with everything he did in life. The adult members of my family were still struggling to find their footing.

"Come on," Claude insisted. "The sooner the better. Unless... you're embarrassed of me?"

I gaped. Embarrassed of *him?* "You've got to be joking."

"Prove it," he replied.

I picked up the phone the next day and called my mom. After the necessary pleasantries, I dropped the bomb, as straightforward as ever: "I started seeing someone a month ago and I like him."

The awkward silence on my mom's end made my stomach churn. I could feel her disapproval oozing through the phone line toward me.

Even though the signatures were in and the decree was pending in the mail, I wasn't "officially" divorced yet. And even though my God-fearing mom had been divorced three times herself, it didn't mean she approved of the practice.

But then she said, "What's his name? Where did you meet? Do you really like him?"

The outpouring of questions eased the tension. I found myself breathing again. Perhaps what I'd thought to be disapproval was in fact wariness. She'd sensed the pain of my first marriage. She'd known I'd been attending therapy again toward the end of it. She didn't want me getting hurt again.

I told her about the compassionate gentleman I'd met at a beautiful restaurant in La Jolla, with his caramel complexion, his beautiful smile, and his warm brown eyes. He was smart, compassionate, tall, muscular, and chivalrous: a software engineer who opened all the doors for me, owned his own home, had all his ducks in a row, and asked to meet my mother. I could hear her smiling as she accepted his invitation, tickled pink that he considered her special enough to want to meet her first.

"Are you happy?" she asked me when I came to pick her up that Sunday for our lunch date with Claude. As we drove into the parking lot, she suddenly asked me if we'd had sex. "Do you have explosions?"

I nearly crashed the car because I was laughing so hard. I'd never heard it termed like that before. I assured her he was giving me "explosions."

"Good," she said sincerely. "You deserve that. Maybe if it works out between you two, you might have a baby and be happy."

Her words came from a place of love and her attempt to show her approval of me moving on with my life. I hugged her. When she met Claude, she interrogated him staunchly and told me he was "fine." It didn't fool me one bit. I could tell she was completely enamored.

My mother approved of our marriage. She was happy for me when I got the position at Walmart, encouraging me to pursue something I liked and was good at. When I told my mom that I was pregnant again, the news filled her with delight. Thirteen weeks in, we were discussing baby names and gushing over baby clothes. Nineteen weeks in, when the doctor informed us of the baby's condition, I called my mom to tell her the news and could barely speak through the tears.

She cried, too, but tried to comfort me anyway. "Ooh, baby, it will be okay," I heard her soft voice say. I'd grown up hearing the phrase *it will be okay* from her so many times that sometimes I still believed it. It was her promise, empty and hopeful, timeless and compassionate.

"Oh, Mom." There are things you can say to a mother that you cannot say to anyone else in the world. "Just as soon as it really feels okay, feels good, then I'm dealing with another situation that I've got to pull myself through. Just when it gets okay, it stops being okay. Why is that?"

"I love you," she said. "You haven't done anything wrong, Connie. It's all God's plan."

It's all God's plan. That was another one of her phrases. One time when I was little, she'd gone to the store with ten dollars in her pocket to buy food for the week for all of us. She'd cut out all the coupons she could and marked all the specials on the supermarket flyer. As she dug into her purse, she found a hundred-dollar bill. Grateful as always, she attributed it to the Lord. *It's all God's plan.*

I pressed the cell phone tightly against my ear, as if doing so would bring my mother physically closer. I could feel the helplessness in her voice, the pain she felt on my behalf. My heart filled a little with the knowledge that she *did* love me. My heart hurt with newfound respect at all the sacrifices she'd made as a mother—sacrifices that I might never have a chance to make. They say you realize a mother's love only once you become a mother yourself. I'd been on the verge of motherhood multiple times and felt so very in love with each little soul I found within me and then lost. Perhaps that had already influenced my perspective.

The pregnancy would be terminated, but that wasn't all. A few days later, my mother called me on my cell phone one morning when I was driving to work with Claude. "I have something to tell you, Connie," she said. "I don't want you to get upset. Everything is going to be okay."

"Mom? What is it?"

She told me that the doctors had diagnosed her with bone marrow cancer and that she'd be going through treatment. I immediately began to sob. Claude pulled the car over and turned down the radio. "Cancer?" I said.

"The doctors say the odds are very good," she said. "Honey, I'm so sorry to tell you during this time. I didn't want you to feel left out and I didn't want you to find out from anyone else…"

"Mom, you did the right thing. Thank you for telling me." I took a deep breath, closing my eyes. I'd thought things couldn't get any worse. I'd been wrong. My mom's call pained me, but it also reminded me that I wasn't alone and neither was she. We all had our crosses to bear. "I love you. It *is* going to be okay."

"I love you too," she said.

. . .

Her love—and those words—were among the things that helped me get through that horrible night in the hospital with my bandaged body and bruised heart. Despite the hardships and the pain—or, perhaps, thanks to them—my relationship with my mother evolved and would continue to evolve throughout my life, going through its own phases just like an emerging butterfly.

She often tells me how blessed she feels about being our mother. "You kids were the highlight of my life. You made me complete. You made me aim higher and do more." Without us, she's told me, she wouldn't be the person she is today. It was worth it. Now that we're grown and scattered, she misses us.

In writing this book, I've learned so much about Evonne, Sylvester, my siblings, and the backstory of my childhood. My mother helped me greatly with her memories and stories throughout the writing process. Along the way, I've come to understand and respect her much more. To this day, she tries her best to show up and be supportive when it matters most. She's survived poverty, abuse, abandonment, and cancer. How can that not make her a fighter?

"You have become a wonderful woman," she told me once. "You grew up with obstacles, eight siblings, and a father who couldn't stay planted. You had a lot of hurt and pain. I don't blame you for being angry."

Perhaps, in some ways, I am more like my mother than I thought.

Evonne had always been lonely. It would take years for me to realize how much she'd truly given up in order to prioritize her nine children. We were all she had, and she loved us more than anything. We forced her to survive, to renew her faith in God, to eventually stand up for herself, and to be her own quiet sort of hero.

At the end of the day, she will always be my mother.

38

THE LOVE OF MY LIFE

On January 16, 2014, Claude and I faced each other in a postcard-perfect setting, surrounded by the golden sand and sapphire sea of St. Lucia. The afternoon breeze whispered through the branches of lush palm trees, tousled my carefully styled hair, and teased the fabric of veil and my mermaid-styled white bridal dress. In front of a white-painted wooden pavilion strung with red and pink flowers, we held hands as a woman minister blessed us.

I said my vows from the heart, savoring every moment, lost in Claude's eyes and finding myself in his love. "You are the best man I've ever met," I confessed to him, fighting to keep back my tears. "I am so grateful, blessed, and happy that God allowed our paths to cross. I didn't know what true love was until I met you. I look forward to a lifetime of joy and happiness with you, knowing that—whatever happens—we will have each other."

Claude took out his cell phone and read his vows to me.

"Every time I see you, my heart melts, and today is no exception. When I look into your eyes it reminds me how blessed I am to have you in my life. You truly are my perfect match and before you ask "WHY?", I am going to tell you…"

And he did. I have these vows, printed out and taped to the inside of my closet door to this day. They remind me of our love for each other, no matter what life might throw at us, and give me strength.

Constance, you are my perfect match because of your:

Loyalty: The faithfulness and commitment you continue to demonstrate in our relationship is truly amazing. Your desire to build a life together on a foundation of trust has eased all the pain and heartache from my past. I am blessed you have healed me and made me whole.

Patience: You know me. You understand me. Yes, I can be a little difficult, stubborn, loud, sarcastic, and sometimes a bit overly frustrated. But with all my faults, you always find the good in me. You have the insight to pick the right battles to hold your ground and constantly strive for the right balance of compromise which challenges me to be a better man. I want to thank you for being my example of true patience in our partnership.

Strength: You are a fighter. You have no problem speaking your mind and will not stand for being pushed around. When adversity comes knocking at your door, you always seem to pave a way and overcome your challenges. You are proud, confident, and successful and I find all those qualities VERY sexy.

Communication: You have the most innovative ways of telling me what's on your mind. I know when the bedroom doors close a bit harder than normal, it's not the wind, but your way of telling me you need a little space. I understand the different looks in your eyes...everything from don't take one step closer, to come comfort me, to it's time to go to bed early tonight. I now realize how you use music, dance, and laughter to let me know what mood you are in. Communication is key in any type of relationship and your willingness to be an open book with your feelings has helped our relationship make it the success it is today.

Creativity: You bring so much excitement to my life. Your free spirit at times has come at odds with my Type A personality; however, you continue to show me life does not need to be lived in the fast lane and I should take the time to enjoy family, friends, and us. You are a creative adventurer always in my business, exploring new crafts, experimenting in the kitchen, and keeping it interesting in the bedroom. I appreciate you and the balance you bring to my world.

Love: You love me and I believe with my entire heart that you do. It feels so good to say that and know that it's true. With all my faults and crazy ways, you continue to focus and articulate what you love in me which keeps me striving to be a better man for you.

Constance Grays, I have been waiting for this day to take my best friend and make her my wife. You are a perfect match, my one, my only, my everything. And we are In It To Win It!

I could not contain my tears then, and my heart nearly burst with the tenderness in his eyes and his voice. A group of local friends surrounded us, cheering and clapping when we kissed. It marked the beginning of our next chapter, our new life together. After the ceremony, we danced our first dance to Luther Vandross' "A House Is Not a Home."

"In it to win it," I whispered to Claude as he held me close, promising him everything that he promised me. No matter what happened, I knew that we could look into each other's eyes—tearful yet trusting—and keep going. We'd been through Hell. We would try to be each other's Heaven.

St. Lucia was a place to remember. When I close my eyes, I can visualize it as if it was yesterday. I recall the sweet gurgling of the turquoise waves as they lapped the sands. I see an impossibly blue sky and mesmerizing mauve sunsets. I remember the happy strain in my legs as I hiked with Claude and a group of new friends along the ridges of those emerald-green volcanic mountains. I remember the warmth of the sun as it soaked into my salt-flecked skin as we splashed around like teenagers and Claude chased me within those crystal waters. I can feel the way my belly ached from laughter after I'd competed in my first-ever potato-sack race. I remember delightful candlelit dinners and how much fun we had dancing to exotic rhythms under the starlight.

We were out of the woods, at least for now. Maybe there would be more dark places in our future, bigger and scarier, but I wasn't afraid anymore. Claude was right: I was a fighter. And I had him. After we'd lost our child, I hadn't expected us to embark on this Caribbean adventure. We had, though; life went on. Claude made sure of that—and he took me along with him. We were grieving and healing and celebrating all at once. We let love give our lives purpose and passion.

Did we live happily ever after? Well, we're happy. And we live. When tomorrow comes, we'll face it together.

I couldn't ask for more.

TODAY AND TOMORROW

2020 is here, and soon I will be forty years old.

I interact with people every day in my community, and it never fails to amaze me how complex and incredible we all are. Just stop and think about it: there are so many stories within each of us. These life stories have molded us into the people we are today. Most of these stories are so remarkable, and they've got the ability to entertain or educate the best of us, yet most of them remain forgotten or unspoken. We don't share much about our stories. We don't ask others for theirs. Isn't it a shame how so many of us take our stories to the grave? Some of us are even shamed by our stories—unable to own them, much less learn from them.

This book tells *my* story, as experienced through my eyes. It's my personal history. Sharing it has been one of the most vulnerable and frightening things I've ever done—but that's the point. In a world of rising walls and unwavering biases, we need to love each other more than ever before. We need to connect with each other as a society. We need to trust each other. To do so, we need to be vulnerable with each other. This begins with a conversation. It goes something like this: "I understand. You're not alone. I've been through rough times, too. I believe in you. You'll be okay."

Multiple times in my life, I've felt lost, afraid, or hopelessly depressed. Once, I almost jumped off the edge and committed suicide. But I didn't. I feel so grateful and glad that I didn't, because I would have never had the chance to experience all that God meant for me to experience throughout my life. I never would have emerged from the pain and resurrected myself as the butterfly that Claude so affectionately calls me. We all have the power—at any given time in our lives—to *choose* to seize the pen and write the rest of our story. We all have the choice between becoming *bitter* or *better* despite past circumstances.

As I survived and thrived despite the obstacle courses that kept popping up in my life, I realized that I am strong. I am powerful. I am more than my circumstances. When I came to that realization, I broke free from toxic cycles and childhood traumas. I opened myself up to opportunities and eventually even found true love and real purpose in my life.

I did not write this book to make you feel sorry for or pity me. For those of you who know me or who thought you knew me, this book was not written to answer questions you might have had about me, either. Although writing this book has been an immensely cathartic experience, I want it to be something even more powerful for *you*. I encourage you to read about my mistakes and learn from them; you don't have to reinvent the wheel. I want you to know that when the darkness takes over your world and it feels like all hope is lost, there's always a way out—*a better way out*. Above all else, I wrote this book to share some valuable messages.

1. You create your own destiny.

For most of my adult life so far, I wasn't passionate about the work I did. Usually I felt that I didn't have a choice. I sometimes found myself living paycheck to paycheck, sharing my savings with needier family members and refusing to reach for a handout. But ever since I was a child, I remember dreaming of a better life. I kept telling myself that I could do more and be more…until eventually I believed it with all my heart.

Even with a vision and a healthy belief system in place, it rarely works out from the get-go. When I'd been with Nathan, I'd tried starting my own business as an event planner, believing it would make me happy. The dream fell flat and I grew disheartened. But I'd felt that itch—the feeling that I could do more, be more—and I knew it would only be a matter of time before I tried again. Claude encouraged me to chase my dreams, time and time again. If it wasn't for him, I would have never applied to Walmart Labs. Maybe I wouldn't have embarked on the journey of becoming a motivational speaker. Maybe I wouldn't have realized that I had the strength to write this book.

I've been at Walmart Labs for five-and-a-half years now, and I really enjoy the variety of my job. I get to wear many hats, but my primary responsibility is to provide employees with a pleasant and fun work environment; whether this involves planning events, coordinating volunteer activities, ensuring employee amenities, or onboarding new hires, I get to bring out the best in myself and promote good vibes and a rich company culture in my workplace. I have faith that this is where I need to be now, contributing and growing as a person. In the meantime, I've expanded these themes of contribution and growth to other facets of my life, including speaking, writing, and philanthropic work.

So what is it that you desire? Are you pursuing it? If not, why not? It's not about feeling entitled or "too good" to work at a certain position (honest work is good work, and that's *always* something to be proud of). It's about chasing what you truly want. We only live once. We only get one shot. This doesn't apply to just the professional or work aspects of your life, of course. It's true for every goal you set.

Seize the opportunities in front of you. Know that sometimes they are temporary; sometimes they serve to just elevate you to the next phase of your life. There is something to be learned from every struggle. You won't emerge from your cocoon if you don't fight. How fast you emerge and how high you fly depend on how fiercely you're willing to fight for success.

Visualize your path and create your own destiny. Your mind is your most powerful muscle. Exercise it.

2.   YOU'LL MAKE MORE ROOM IN YOUR HEART BY FORGIVING.

If you want to live a happy life, learn from the past—and then let it go. You don't have to forget...but you need to forgive.

I came of age in a wilderness of beer bottles, domestic violence, and welfare stamps. I was deafened by the screams of babies, the tears of an abused mother, and the slurs of a haunted alcoholic. The two adults who were meant as my guides through this jungle of life were little more than children themselves, and I lost sight of them more times than they lost sight of me. I had eight other siblings to fend for. For most of my childhood, my survival tactic was to harness my own free will, my self-control, and my focus on the little pockets of sunshine that lanced through the trees.

Growing up, I'd always thought things would be different. I believed that I had the tenacity to carve out my own destiny and create my own magic—and that I didn't need magic beans or fairy godmothers or knights in shining armor to rescue me. I carried the hope inside me like a tiny sun that warmed me from the inside out—like secret knowledge that everything will be okay in the end; if it's not okay, it's not the end. After college, after Jordan, I felt toughened in some ways and bruised in others. I was still young, strong, and determined; the sun in my heart burned strong.

My time with Nathan brought back much of the darkness. For a long while, I was angry at Nathan for not having the strength of character that I wanted him to have. I was angry at my mother—a mortal woman who tried to love her big, broken family as best she could with what little she had—for what I perceived as unsupportive or even selfish behavior. I was angry at my body for betraying me in so many ways for so many years. I was angry at my father for disappearing from my life multiple times for many years. I was angry at the world for smacking me back to the ground after I'd fought so hard to stand on my feet. I was angry at God for taking my children from me. I was angry at myself because I felt I wasn't enough.

But you must realize that at the end of the day, the world owes you nothing. At the end of the day, however, you owe yourself a world's worth of compassion. Anger emerges from fear. And fear—if you don't face it—will kill you, wrapping you tighter and tighter in its grip until you suffocate. So deal with the anger. Accept the forgiveness. Seek the peace.

To do all that, you begin with yourself.

3. YOU'RE NOT ALONE.

I am grateful for everyone I've met in my life, including the people who hurt me the most. I am thankful for the classmates who ridiculed me as an epileptic, for the men who dishonored and pained me, for the colleagues or managers who were blinded by their prejudices, for those who betrayed or judged me for being myself. They have taught me how it feels to be judged, taught me what I will stand for, taught me to create my standards, and made me further appreciate the people in my life who embody love, humanity, and integrity. If it wasn't for them, I would have never discovered my true strength, my core values, and my high standards. I never would have stirred free from my cocoon. They say that the transformation process begins when the pain of staying stagnant overrides the fear of change.

There will be people in your life who tell you that you can't do things. Do them anyway. Black women are a minority that society seeks to stigmatize in terms of both race and gender—and because of that we are most likely to go unnoticed and unheard. There will be people in your life who would prefer that you were tucked away in some corner, mummified like a butterfly caught in a spider's web. Speak anyway. Be noticed. Break free. Defy everyone and anyone who seeks to make you *less than*. Defy them, above all, by proving yourself and fighting for your dreams.

My tenacity and my will to succeed propelled me to survive and even thrive during tough times. But you know what? I was *never* alone, even though many times it felt like it. Many incredible people in my life helped me both directly and indirectly, either as providers or role models or friends.

With very little money, no steadfast partner, and a perpetually breaking heart, my mom took care of me and my siblings as best she could when

I was growing up. My badass grandmother never forgot my birthday and made time to spend time with me; I know that some of the strength I have now is a direct result of my time with her. My brother Derrick often protected me, and my half-brother Andre stopped me from committing suicide. Chris Daniels and Mr. Delgado inspired me. Uncle Kahari, Aunt Ledesi, Amara, Diedre, Nala, and Sanaa stepped in when my dad stepped out. My friends supported me emotionally and physically throughout my childhood and adulthood, whether I needed a room to sleep in or a shoulder to cry on. Samantha, Aaliyah, Riley, Sienna, Seiko, Damion, Natalie, and Jasmine remain especially close to my heart. Even my dad's ministry work allowed me to attend Point Loma with a discount and lessened my college loans. Then there's Claude, of course, who inspires me to be my best self…and loves me for it unconditionally.

Claude and I both come from difficult backgrounds that included poverty, bad role models, traumatic childhoods, and personal tragedies. We both grew up Christian, but we slowly found ourselves becoming more spiritual and less religious. I'm pretty sure there are churches out there that are exemplary—as transparent and compassionate as they are pious—but Claude and I were not there. In the churches we attended, we never felt like we belonged; we participated, prayed, and paid our monthly tithes, but we didn't know where the money was going and we didn't have faith in our leaders. We chose to seek and worship a God who embodies love and acceptance. All of these things prompted us to find another way to give and actively participate in our community

That's how Elevate Foundation was born. Our purpose is to help rebuild communities, uplift individuals, and inspire others to do the same. For us, success means that we've changed other people's lives through our acts of giving. We know we've done well when we see someone seizing those opportunities, succeeding, and then paying it forward in turn.

4. DON'T GIVE UP ON LOVE AND LIFE.

So is this it? Am I done? Am I perfect?

No, no, and no. Self-improvement is a lifelong challenge. It's a never-ending evolution, a butterfly transformation story where you shed a layer of darkness each time and can choose to fly to greater heights each day. I can be very stubborn, sometimes too blunt, and I'm a work in progress in so many ways. Looking back, however, I count my blessings and feel glad of how far I've come. I've grown and will continue to do so. I'm spending more time with my family, reconnecting with my sisters and mother. We're all adults now, so it's a different sort of journey: heartbreaking and beautiful and not always easy, but absolutely worthwhile.

All in all, we're doing all right. Mia is stable on her medication. She lives in a halfway home now where she's got her own studio apartment. She's still a sweetheart at her core, attending church each Sunday with Aunt Ledesi and often reaching out to the rest of us. Andre resides in Atlanta with his girlfriend; he's following in my dad's footsteps by attending a school of theology to become a minister. Derrick got a divorce, visits his kid as much as he can, and lives with his new girlfriend in Las Vegas. He's a good dad; he teared up when his daughter got her driver's license, because he realized how fast kids grow up. Over in San Diego, Michael is raising his daughter as a dependable single dad, and Jeremiah moved in with his girlfriend and is trying out a new side hustle in the food industry.

Big-hearted Xavier is happily married to a nurse and has made a good name for himself in the insurance market; Claude and I are the proud godparents of his cute and sassy two-year-old daughter. He reminds me most of Uncle Kahari; he tries to keep the Grays together and close. Laila, likewise married, has also attained a steady paycheck and a darling daughter. Alyssa, married and with a lovely daughter (also our goddaughter) and stepson, has been steadily promoted at her bank job in Vegas. She shares my love for creativity; in her free time, she paints and meditates.

My dad never did really take up the mantle of fatherhood. He's popped up a couple of times in my life since, coming and going like a hurricane that promises winds of change but just leaves desolation and isolation in its wake. He isn't open to changing—perhaps with even the very best of intentions, he is unable to change. I've realized that the people who are meant to be in our lives are the ones who stay. I've learned that I owe it to myself to protect my heart and keep my distance. I feel that I've had enough toxicity, drama, and dysfunctionality in my life.

I blame him for all the suffering he has caused me, but I also blame him for making me this fearless, this fierce, this independent, and this smart. If it wasn't for his suboptimal parenting, I wouldn't have cultivated the strength within me to get through worse obstacles late in life. Though it's unrealistic to forget all that he did and did not do, I have forgiven my father. I worked on that for years, finally realizing that forgiveness meant putting myself first. Refusing to forgive someone is like drinking poison and hoping the other person will die. How can I expect to embrace the future if I don't first release the past? How can I expect to fly if I don't break the shackles from my ankles? Martin Luther King, Jr. once said, "Darkness cannot drive out darkness; only light can do that. Hate cannot drive out hate; only love can do that."

My mother and I have gotten closer. I feel that she's understood how much it means to me to have a close relationship with her. She was in remission for five years before the cancer returned, and then she fought it back off. Her levels have since stabilized, lifting a heavy weight from all our hearts.

Claude and I are happily married. Letting go of our daughter was one of the darkest times of my life. When Claude and I went to the mall weeks later to buy some new clothes, we walked by the maternity store where I'd bought all my clothes when I'd been pregnant. I saw a woman waddling out, looking so pregnant that her water may have been ready to break then and there. I began sobbing so hard that we had to leave the mall and go home. We've since tried to have another child and I had another miscarriage, my fifth such loss. I've come to accept that having children isn't my destiny.

We work hard and live a comfortable life; we just moved into a new home. It's farther from the city with a lush yard and beautiful views, I couldn't love it more. We both still work at Walmart Labs among a community of fantastic people. We both pursue our passions as speakers and writers and givers. We're slowly and steadily traveling the world just as we'd always dreamed about, checking off India, Maldives, the Bahamas, Canada, Jamaica, and more off our bucket list. We both have found purpose in giving back to society, realizing that we would have never succeeded had others not given us our own share of inspiration, opportunities, and hope.

Claude was my first date on Match.com, and he's been my last date since. He is the love of my life. Getting to know him did not mark the end of my adventures or ordeals—and who truly knows what the future holds?—but knowing him makes the journey a better one.

5. **You're stronger than you think you are.**

We are products of our past but also the creators of our purpose. We cannot go back and change whatever has happened to us or around us, but we always have a choice in how we will live today. We always have a choice about what we will dream up for tomorrow. If I've given hope to even one person out there who is going through similar experiences, then I consider this book to be a success.

Repeat after me: *I am strong. I am powerful. I am more than my circumstances.*

Life is what you make of it.

A Few Parting Words...

PLEASE LEAVE A REVIEW!

Thank YOU, dear reader, for taking the time to read my story. If you enjoyed this book, please don't forget to give it a review on Amazon, Goodreads, and/or on the retailer's site from which you purchased or borrowed it. Even just a couple of words or a sentence makes a difference and helps to spread the word. Others will benefit from your experience and your insight. I truly appreciate your support.

A SECRET SURPRISE JUST FOR YOU...

I've uploaded a gallery of photographs on my website, which depict various phases of my life. Only the people who have read this book know about this page...I hope you find it interesting! https://theemerg-ingbutterfly.com/gallery

SIGN UP AND JOIN ME ON MY NEXT CHAPTER!

This memoir is only the beginning of my next chapter in life. There is much to say and much to do, so stay tuned for upcoming books and interviews and motivational talks. Sign up on www.constancegjones. com, and I'll notify you about new releases. No spamming—I promise. And your information won't ever be shared with a third party.

WEBSITE: http://constancegjones.com

WEBSITE: http://theemergingbutterfly.com

GOODREADS: goodreads.com/constancegjones

FACEBOOK: https://www.facebook.com/iamconstancejones

INSTAGRAM: https://www.instagram.com/constanceg.jones

TWITTER: https://twitter.com/iamemerging

ELEVATE FOUNDATION: http://elevate.foundation

Author Bio

Constance G. Jones is a San Diego native, an avid reader, and a storyteller. She earned her bachelor's degree in Management and Organizational Communications from Point Loma Nazarene University and has since worked in administration, public relations, and career services; most recently, she serves as a site manager at Walmart Global eCommerce. In 2016, Constance founded Elevate Foundation with her husband, Claude, driven by their personal mission to make an impact in their local community and inspire others to do the same. *Emerging Butterfly: A Memoir* is Constance's debut book.

CPSIA information can be obtained
at www.ICGtesting.com
Printed in the USA
LVHW091933030220
645687LV00010B/243/J